MW01528750

Hallie's Comet

To Audra,
Best,
Denise Dietz

Hallie's Comet

Denise Dietz

Five Star • Waterville, Maine

This novel is a work of fiction. Names, characters, places and incidents are either the product of the author's imagination, or, if real, used fictitiously.

First Edition
First Printing: April 2004

Published in 2004 in conjunction with Tekno Books and Ed Gorman.

Set in 11 pt. Plantin by Christina S. Huff.

Printed in the United States on permanent paper.

Library of Congress Cataloging-in-Publication Data

Dietz, Denise.
Hallie's comet : a paranormal romance mystery / by—1st ed.
p. cm.
ISBN 1-59414-102-9 (hc : alk. paper)
1. Women artists—Fiction. 2. Photographers—Fiction. 3. Reincarnation—Fiction. 4. Colorado—Fiction. I. Title.
PS3554.I368H35 2004
813′.54—dc22 2003065567

This book is dedicated to Denise Little . . .
one of the best editors (and nicest people)
in the publishing biz.

Acknowledgments

During the ten years it took me to research and write my 1893–1925 saga, *The Rainbow's Foot,* I discovered more juicy tidbits than I could possibly use in one novel, even a long novel, so I decided to write *Hallie's Comet.* My pilgrimage through Cripple Creek, Colorado, was aided and abetted by the encouragement of Mary Ellen Johnson, Lynn Whitacre, Fran Baker, Jasmine Cresswell, Maggie Osborne, and, especially, Colorado's Penrose Library. Writing *Hallie's Comet* would not have been possible without the loving support of the incredibly talented Gordon Aalborg, who taught me the real meaning of the word "romance."

Chapter One

A buckboard careened down the street, clods of earth from its wheels spawning loam-crusted surf.

Hallie O'Brien choked back a cry. She rarely drove a car. When she did, its tires spun down boulevards or parkways or fume-filled expressways.

So why did she envision a runaway horse and wagon? And why did she envision a street paved with dirt rather than tar? Ruts rather than potholes?

There was no logical reason. The TV had remained silent for days and she hadn't seen a movie in months. Just like her other offbeat visions, this one had been spontaneous, unprovoked by outside influences.

Drawing a deep, calming breath, she glanced around the living room until her gaze touched upon her workbench. Circa 1890, the bench had been used by a harness repairer.

There! That must be the answer.

But could an antique workbench generate hallucinations? Not really. Not unless a telepathic poltergeist lurked inside. Or maybe the workbench had leapt out of a Stephen King novel. With a shrug of her slender shoulders, Hallie scrutinized the well-crafted piece of mahogany.

It had four drawers down the right side and a slightly raised platform upon which she could rest one weary leg at a time. Spread out across its surface were tubes of acrylic paint, two sketch pads, a bottle of linseed oil, a can of turpentine, a palette knife, and several paintbrushes. Amid the organized clutter was a radio, circa 1990. Today the radio droned vintage Motown and the Temptations sang about how beauty was only skin-deep.

Hallie shifted her gaze to the portrait she had just painted. She prayed that this man's beauty wasn't skin-deep. She wanted his soul to match his eyes.

" 'I dream my painting, and then I paint my dreams,' " she said, quoting Vincent van Gogh. Stepping away from the easel, located smack-dab in the middle of her sparsely furnished Bayside apartment, she attempted a grin that was, she suspected, a mite sheepish. "I sure dreamed up this painting, Marianne."

"Hallie O'Brien! Are you telling me that your drop-dead gorgeous man doesn't exist?"

"Only in my dreams." Hallie had rescued her brother's business shirt from his giveaway carton. Knotting the shirttails above her paint-spattered jeans, she watched her sister-in-law's brow furrow.

Marianne snapped her fingers. "I know," she said. "He looks like Mel Gibson."

"He does not."

"He does too. The hair's different, but that smile . . ." Marianne sighed dramatically. "That mouth belongs to Mel."

Hallie twirled one of her shiny dark curls around her index finger. "I wish that mouth belonged to me," she blurted, a blush staining her cheekbones.

"What's black and white and red all over?" asked Marianne, her voice filled with amusement.

"An embarrassed zebra?"

"Nope. An embarrassed Hallie. You needn't be ashamed of your sexual impulses, girl."

"Give me a break! What is this? Psychology 101?" She

fisted her hands into a funnel and brought the improvised bullhorn to her lips. "Alice W. O'Brien," she monotoned. "Twenty-seven-year-old maiden. Can't find her dream man. So she paints the man of her dreams."

"Maiden?" Marianne patted her French braid, searching for a stray wisp or tendril. There weren't any. "Why not call yourself a vestal virgin?"

"A vestal virgin," Hallie said, "watches the sacred fire perpetually kept burning on Vesta's alter. Vesta was a Roman goddess who . . ."

She paused as new images came to mind.

A night sky filled with fire. Soon the horse-drawn wagon would crush the man and woman . . .

"No!" An anguished moan lapped at the back of her throat. "Watch out!"

"What? Where? Another spider?" Marianne darted anxious glances around the room.

"It was a daddy longlegs and he's been evicted." Hallie's mind raced as she tried to invent a plausible excuse for her warning. She didn't want to admit that vivid visions had plagued her all summer. "You almost jostled my masterpiece, Marianne," she managed, nodding toward the painting.

"Hallie, I haven't moved one inch. I was listening to your ancient history lesson. History lessons run in your family. Anyway, I thought a vestal virgin was another name for a chaste woman."

"It is. Please stop talking about virgins, vestal or otherwise." Feeling like a demented hitchhiker, she jerked her thumb toward the crimson-cushioned couch where her nephew Jefferson was napping. The two-year-old's cheek rested against an overstuffed purple dinosaur, and she began to contemplate a painting. Vermilion, umber, a smidgen of Prussian blue. And purple.

"Are you afraid we might corrupt Jeff's morals?" Marianne winked. "Elmo introduced the V-word this morning, on 'Sesame Street.' You're a nineteenth-century woman stuck inside a time warp, my friend."

Hallie didn't react. Her so-called time warp was a family joke.

Walking toward the couch, she said, "Jeff's looking more and more like his dad every day, a miniature Neil Diamond O'Brien. Speaking of Neil, how's my prolific brother?"

"Thriving. Successful. Very."

"You sound cynical, Marianne."

"I didn't mean to. It's just . . ." Her voice trailed off as she heaved a deep, sincere sigh.

Trying to hold her breath and speak at the same time, Hallie said, "What's the matter?"

"Nothing major. Please don't look so scared. I love your brother. He loves me. It's just that Neil's success breeds social events. Uppah crust, my deah, uppah crust."

Hallie studied her sister-in-law's tall form. Even sporting an eight—or was it nine?—month belly bulge, Marianne could easily grace the cover of *Vogue*. On the other hand, Hallie could probably pose for *Jack and Jill*. Not that her body lacked curves. However, her riot of ebony curls and dark eyes seemed to defy the aging process. She had been asked on more than one occasion to produce ID at her own champagne gallery openings.

Even her name. Her big brother Neil, a toddler when she was born, couldn't pronounce Alice, so Alice morphed into Hallie. She'd just as soon forget her middle name.

She probably looked young because she looked innocent.

Oh, she'd been kissed and stroked, she wasn't *that* innocent, but she'd always managed to stop before it got out of hand.

Bottom line: she didn't want sex without love. Maybe she *was* stuck in some nineteenth-century time warp. Or maybe she was waiting for her dream man to come along and sweep her off her feet. Or maybe she wanted to remain faithful to the man in her painting, the man who didn't exist.

A wistful yearning stabbed through her. "Neil's success breeds children, my dear," she said, striving for humor. "I've lost count. Is this new baby number five or six?"

"Five. What's wrong with having kids?" Marianne's voice sounded defensive.

"Nothing. I was joking. And I've kept count, honest. Tina Turner O'Brien, Barbra Streisand O'Brien, Madonna O'Brien, and Jefferson Airplane O'Brien."

"Thank goodness Neil let me name Jeff. Your brother wanted to call him Wonder, after Stevie, but I put my foot down." Marianne glanced down at her feet. "Do you think my ankles look swollen?"

Hallie shook her head emphatically, the motion causing her curls to bounce. "Why don't you sit, Marianne?"

"Why don't you?"

"Because I'm still 'adrenalized.' I've been working on that portrait nonstop. It's exciting and scary and . . . damn. I just said something stupid, didn't I?"

"No."

"Yes, I did. If a picture is worth a thousand words, your face is worth a bazillion."

Marianne paced between the couch and matching love seat, her sneakers carefully avoiding the paint-spattered sail-cloth that dominated a patch of uncarpeted floor. The sail-cloth was Hallie's seabed. When she felt stressed, she called it her B'rer Alice laughin' place.

" 'Fess up," Hallie urged.

"You're creative while I'm pregnant."

"Having a baby is more creative than painting pictures, and you know it." If she hadn't been so struck by her sister-in-law's anguished expression, she would have grinned. Only Marianne could wear jogging sneakers with a rhinestone-studded maternity dress and still manage to look chic. "C'mon, kiddo, 'fess up."

"Jeff's impossible to potty-train. Why are girls so much easier than boys?"

"You're upset over diapers? Not!"

Marianne halted mid-stride. With the intensity of a guru, she contemplated her shoelaces. "Your brother loves Wall Street but hates commuting," she said, the words coming out in a rush. "He wants to move closer to work. Do you know how much it costs to live in Manhattan? We'd have to sell the kids. I want to stay in Bayside. My house may be old, but it's big, and I can watch my garden grow. I just planted daffodils, beets, carrots and tomatoes."

"Daffodils. Yum."

"At least three times a week I drive to the city and meet Neil at his office. The kids have begun to call the baby-sitter Mommy. When we attend those upper-crust gatherings, Hallie, somebody always asks me what I do. You know, what I do for a living? I've been tempted to answer airline pilot, but since I'm always pregnant I didn't think that would fly. I've tried domestic goddess, but all they hear is the word domestic and they think I work for a cleaning service. 'Robin Hood and His Merry Band of Maids.' "

"Wow, that's great. Did you make it up?"

"Yes."

"You could be in advertising, Marianne."

"Right. I can see the yellow pages ad. 'We steal from the rich and give to the poor and wash windows.' "

"I'd hire you. My place could use a good cleaning, especially the windows. I'm a tad broke right now, but I'd write you an IOU." Her finger jabbed the air, forming an I, an O and a U. "There's more than enough dust on my TV screen."

"It's not funny, Hallie. A snooty lady asked what I did and I said chief cook and bottle washer. Big mistake. I could practically hear their gossipy whispers. 'Poor Neil. His wife watches soaps all day. What do they talk about at night?' "

"Don't fret, Marianne. They're jealous. Obviously, you and Neil do more than talk."

"At our last wingding, I settled for housewife and managed to endure their pity."

"Confusion, not pity. They're so dull-witted they thought you were the wife of a house."

"I'm big as a house." Marianne pirouetted. At the same time, she hugged her bulging belly.

"Big as an apartment," Hallie corrected.

"Mansion. Oops. Jeff's awake, and he's about to entertain us with infant profanity. Madonna says she's been teaching him the 'baddest word ever.' I've got to use your bathroom. Please keep my son away from Mel Gibson. His lips haven't dried yet."

Hallie's heels supported her rump as she knelt by the couch. "Hi, neph," she said. "Would you like some milk and cookies?"

"Doody cookies. Doody diaper."

"Oh, dear." She unsnapped his rompers. "You're not even wet, Jeff."

"Doody Barney," he said gleefully, clutching his stuffed dinosaur. "Doody milk, doody bottle, gimme."

"Oh, I get it. Madonna. The baddest word ever. Let's learn a new word, okay? How about Gabriel?"

Gabriel? Where on earth did that come from?

Hallie's gaze lit upon Marianne's purse and diaper bag,

both tossed negligently on top of the love seat. Toys spilled from the diaper bag, mostly miniature musical instruments, including one horn. Gabriel blew his horn. A feeble explanation, but it would have to do.

Because she didn't know anyone named Gabriel.

The man in her painting could be Gabriel. Although his face and upper body manifested great strength, there was an angelic quality to his eyes. He looked young yet ageless, solid yet yielding, decisive yet reasonable.

Good grief, she was imbuing a man she'd never met with qualities that didn't exist. At least they didn't exist in her world of inflated male egos and artistic temperaments.

She had never painted a dream man before. She didn't even attempt realistic portraiture, having developed a style devoted to pure Impressionism, influenced by her three idols: Picasso, Degas and van Gogh.

"My sister paints the three bars," Neil had once said, inflecting his voice with a Davy Crockett drawl.

"Bars? Oh, *bears!* Your accent is ghastly," she had reprimanded, weaving her hand through her dark curls. "You sound like Elvis with a bad cold. And if you're talking Papa Bar, Mama Bar, and Baby Bar, I'm not Goldilocks, not even close."

"I didn't mean bear bars, Hallie. I meant barns, bargains, and a ballerina's barre."

Her brother's witty wisecrack had some merit, thought Hallie, since she sometimes borrowed her father's minivan and drove through New York State, halting to sketch barns, cows, street fairs and auctions. In fact, she had found her workbench at a farm auction and bought it for a song.

Speaking of songs, the Temptations were singing about how they wished it would rain. Hallie heard the muted growl of thunder. Soon the Temptations would get their wish.

Her gaze touched upon her latest canvas, propped against a big-screen TV, blocking the screen. She had abandoned that canvas to paint her dream man, but her work-in-progress depicted several ballerinas caught in a rhythmical wave of motion. She often attended rehearsals for the Dance Theatre of Harlem, then used her preliminary drawings to create expressions of spiritual ecstasy. One pretentious art critic had labeled her "the female Degas."

A scowl creased her brow. That same critic wouldn't call another artist the male Degas, would he?

"Sorry, Jeff, your auntie was daydreaming. Where were we? Milk and cookies, right? You're such a good boy." She scooped up her nephew and carried him to the portable playpen. "Your bottle's in the fridge, and I bought a box of animal crackers. Lions and tigers and bars, oh my."

"Doody cackers." Jeff snatched up a piece of soft flannel. Looking like Linus in "Peanuts," he said, "Curity blankie."

Wish I had a "curity" blanket, Hallie thought. *Maybe it would cure my spur-of-the-moment visions*. Aloud, she said, "I'll be back straightaway, little love."

She walked into her kitchen. Just like her living room, dining room and bedroom, it was sparsely furnished. One of her cow paintings dominated the east wall. A sturdy butcher-block table and four wicker-backed chairs looked lost in a sea of decorative, kiln-baked tile. A microwave and knife sharpener had been housewarming gifts. Her cedar-scented cabinets accommodated six crystal goblets and six china dinner plates. Her silverware drawer held an array of plastic forks, knives, spoons and wooden chopsticks, all scrounged from the Chinese takeout she habitually ordered.

It wasn't that she expected to leave on the spur of the moment. She merely wanted to purchase items uniquely individual, possibly one of a kind. And if that meant eating with plastic utensils or placing a thick mattress on top of her handwoven Indian rug until she found the perfect bed, so be it.

For twenty-seven years, minus three years in Paris when she had studied at the Academia de la Grande Chaumiere, Hallie had lived with her parents. Both were employed by the New York City Board of Education. Her father, Shamus, taught music appreciation and coached the high school football team. Her mother, Josie, taught history. Craving independence, Hallie had searched high and low for the perfect apartment. Like Neil, she loved the vibrant energy of Manhattan. Like Marianne, she preferred to live in the more laid-back suburbs.

It was Marianne who had discovered Hallie's duplex, located at the end of a cul-de-sac, next door to a country club. From her back windows, she could see the manicured golf course, and the only sounds that occasionally pierced her concentration were the muffled oaths from golfers who'd boogied or bogeyed or whatever the heck it was called. She didn't know diddly about golf. She played tennis. Oh, she wasn't a pro, not even close, but she could hold her own against most athletic amateurs.

Damn, she'd better stop daydreaming—again!—and start behaving like a mommy. Marianne, at Hallie's insistence, was leaving Jeff overnight so that he could have some "quality time away from his sisters." Meanwhile, Marianne would drive to the city for yet another upper-crust gathering.

"Hallie?"

"Yes?" She turned away from the refrigerator, where she'd been reaching for Jeff's clown-shaped bottle. "Ohmigosh, Marianne, what's the matter?"

"My water broke."

"What?"

"Which word didn't you understand?"

"Okay, sweetie, let's not panic. We'll simply call Neil, your doctor, the hospit—"

"My hospital's Mt. Sinai." Marianne winced, then grabbed a chair for support. "I don't think I'll have time to make it from Bayside to Manhattan."

"No problem. We'll find a hospital that's closer."

"And when, may I ask, did you buy a car?"

"My bike is parked against the living room wall. Its tires are a tad low, but there's a bicycle pump in the front hall clos—"

"You want me to ride your *handlebars?*"

"Not a good idea, huh?"

"Unless there's a delivery room inside the country club, I think you'll have to play midwife."

"Don't be silly. I've seen movies. TV. It takes hours and hours to have a baby."

Marianne's mouth gave rise to a lopsided smile. "This is my fifth kid, kiddo. I'm primed like a pump."

"You're joking. You're not joking."

"Sorry, but I think you've got to hold down the fort until the paramedics arrive. Or my doctor."

"Doctor," Hallie repeated, dazed. She consulted her authentic Coca-Cola wall clock. Then her gaze shifted past the clock, as if she could see through the wall and onto the golf course. "It's only three-thirty. Don't doctors play golf? Sure they do. So it's really quite simple. I'll just step outside and—"

"Hallie, have you looked through a window recently? It's raining cats and dogs."

"Damn the Temptations. They wished for rain. Okay, scratch the golfing doctor. I'll give Jeff his bottle, call your obstetrician, then nine-double-one. Let's see. I'll need hot water and a knife. Rats! I don't have a real knife, just plastic, and I don't think chopsticks will cut it."

"Cut what?"

"The umbilical cord. I'm not the least bit nervous, Marianne, honest. I have a knife sharpener and a palette knife and a copy of last Sunday's *New York Times*."

"Oh, great. Do you plan to fill in the crossword puzzle while you wait?"

"Haven't you seen movies? They always use newspapers. The pages are sterile or something. Steve McQueen once used a leather bomber jacket, and in that movie about med students, you know, the one where they're always working on corpses? . . . Anyway, they used a checkered tablecloth, at least I think they did."

"I'm glad you're not nervous, Hallie."

"Hush. Get into bed."

"You don't have a bed."

"Okay, get into mattress."

"Into mattress?"

"On. I meant on. Hurry. No. Don't hurry. Walk slowly. I'd help you, but I have to fill a pan with water and . . ."

Hallie blinked. *Not now,* she thought as another vision came to mind.

A child clad in knickers was preparing to light a wood-burning stove. In her hand she clutched a box of matches.

"Your pains are very close together," Hallie said, her voice somewhat sluggish. "He won't get here in time."

"Who? The doctor? Neil?"

"No. Gabriel."

"Who on earth is Gabriel?"

"Get into bed, Mama Scarlet!"

"Who's Mama Scarlet?" Face scrunched, Marianne emitted a long, drawn-out groan. Then another.

That cleared away the mist that had momentarily obscured Hallie's vision. "Scoot," she said to Marianne. "I'll take care of everything, I promise."

True to her word, Hallie took care of everything. She even tossed her palette knife into a pot of boiling water and fished it out with chopsticks.

"The Temptations wished it would rain and now they're singing 'My Girl.' " On her knees, Hallie pressed a cold washcloth against Marianne's brow. "What do you want, sweetie? A boy or a girl?"

"Neil. I want Neil."

"Let's sing."

"You're tone-deaf."

"Who's listening?"

"Me. The baby."

"Okay. You can be my backup."

"Backup?"

"Right. Sing the do-rah-rahs."

"What?"

"Which word didn't you understand?" Hallie teased. "Never mind. You can play my orchestra."

"Have you lost your mind?"

"Pant, Marianne. Pretend you're blowing into a flute."

"I don't *believe* this."

"Pant, dammit! My girl," Hallie sang, "talkin' 'bout my girl, oh-oh."

"Ooooh . . ."

"If it's a girl we'll call her Temptation. Where the hell are the paramedics? They probably got stuck in a traffic jam."

"I like Temptation, Hallie, but Neil gets to name this one since I chose Jeff. *Oooohhhh.*"

While the clock ticked away the minutes, everything seemed to occur in slow-motion, as if Hallie aimed her finger at a VCR's fast forward button but kept hitting the pause button by mistake. Desperate, suggesting that Marianne blow a pitch pipe, a bugle, an oboe, even a bassoon, begging her to push and pant, Hallie was dimly aware that the baby arrived in time to hear the Supremes. "Stop," they sang, "in the name of love."

Neil arrived in time to name his new daughter.

The obstetrician, tracked down by his service, arrived in time to congratulate Hallie on a job well done.

A couple of paramedics toted Marianne and the newly christened Shania Twain O'Brien toward a curbside ambulance. Soon the strident hum of sirens pierced the neighborhood's rain-shrouded curtain, and Hallie found a few precious moments to wonder why she'd handled the baby's delivery so efficiently.

She remembered calling Marianne "Mama Scarlet" and telling her that he, Gabriel, wouldn't be back in time. And although Shania's emergence had been somewhat kaleidoscopic, Hallie had performed competently. The palette knife had been too whippy, too bendable, so she didn't dare cut the umbilical cord. But she had hummed a hymn, "There Is Sunshine in Your Soul," a hymn she didn't even know she knew. She had endured Marianne's bone-crushing grip, cooled her brow with a wet cloth, and promised help would arrive any minute.

As if she'd done it before.

Chapter Two

The woman who posed for Gabriel Quinn wasn't beautiful. She had a moon-shaped face, and Gabe wanted to strangle the beautician who'd tortured those soft brown curls into what looked like a frizzy Orphan Annie wig.

Perm, my eye, he thought. *It's a permutation.*

Stifling his irrational anger, he extracted flowers from a cut-glass vase, shook the stems free of water, then wove them together and placed the circlet on top of Anne McFadden's head.

Perfect! Red rosebuds brought out the sheen on her carmine lips, violet pansies darkened the baby blue of her eyes, and the flowers effectively disguised what she'd tearfully called a bad hair day.

"I'm having a bad hair day, Mr. Quinn," she'd said, after changing into her hula dance costume. "Why, oh, why did Johnny insist I have my picture taken?"

"Because he's stationed at a military post overseas and he wants to fulfill his fantasies until he returns," Gabe had responded cheerfully, watching a vivid blush rouge Anne's cheekbones. Some of his clients were brazenly provocative. Others squirmed, cringed, or tried to hide their lovely assets.

Anne McFadden was a cringer.

"Have you ever been overseas, Mr. Quinn?" she had asked, pouncing like a cat on the word "overseas" rather than "fantasies."

"I was a photojournalist, Ms. McFadden. I covered

combat situations in India, Pakistan, Mozambique, Northern Ireland, and numerous other locales."

Silent, she had contemplated his reply while she paced up and down the small platform. Now, a minute or two later, she stopped short and thunked her forehead with the heel of her hand.

"Gabriel Q," she breathed. "I knew you looked familiar. Didn't *Newsweek* write an article about you?"

"Yes. Shall we get started?"

"The article included pictures and I thought you looked like a movie star." This time her cheeks flushed crimson. "Why did you quit photojournalism, Mr. Quinn?"

"You're procrastinating, Ms. McFadden."

"I'd really like to know. And please call me Anne."

Momentarily, Gabe considered making some dumb remark about how he'd rather shoot pretty girls. Instead, he blurted out the truth. "When I covered my last conflict," he said, gesturing toward his left leg, "a piece of artillery exploded near me and flying shrapnel hit my knee. But that's the chance one takes. During Desert Storm I could have stubbed my toe on a land mine."

"Do you suppose they have many land mines overseas?" she asked, her face scrunched up with fearful anxiety.

Gabe held back a sigh. He should have made his pretty girl remark, but he found it difficult to lie, even in the best—or worst—of circumstances.

"There's probably lots of land," he replied with a wink, hoping his wink would reassure her. "However, we have more mines right here in Colorado. Gold mines, silver mines. Have you ever seen those wonderful black-and-white photos of the men who worked the Cripple Creek gold mines?"

"Yes. Johnny drove me to Cripple Creek before he left. We toured the museum and even walked through the Old

Homestead. You know, the parlor house? It wasn't at all what I expected. I mean, it could have been a boardinghouse. I mean . . ." Her voice trailed off as yet another flush suffused her cheeks. Then, out of the blue, she said, "You look like Mel Gibson, Mr. Quinn."

Gabe tried not to grimace. Good ol' Mel. Sometimes Gabe wondered if people told Mel Gibson he looked like Gabriel Quinn.

"Please call me Gabe," he said, scrutinizing Anne through the lens of his 35-mm camera. The flowers subdued her frizzy hair and her face looked fine. She had stopped cringing. However, her body was unresponsive, stiff as an ironing board. No. Stiffer. Gabe's old board tended to give way when he pressed his white slacks and blue denim shirt, the clothes he wore while playing boudoir photographer.

His fiancée, Jenn, didn't care for what she called "Gabriel Q's preposterous profession." He had tried to explain that women were now seeking a sophisticated image, slightly more risqué than the traditional portrait. Many couples wanted to stop the clock forever with tastefully created, provocative poses, more suitable for memory lane than the wedding album.

Despite his fiancée's derisive opinion, Gabe earned a goodly sum at his preposterous profession. His bank account was growing by leaps and bounds, and even if he couldn't leap and bound anymore, he had submitted his résumé to several magazines. And the White House. After all, there was no reason why he couldn't become the president's personal photographer. "If you drop a dream, it breaks," he told Jenn.

"Analyzing dreams is like investigating air," she shot back. "I prefer reality."

"So do I. That's why I'm a boudoir photographer."

Gabe's waiting room displayed the usual copies of *Vogue*,

Cosmo, *GQ* and *People*, but he always included the latest Victoria's Secret catalogue. "Vicky's Exquisite Skivvies," a nickname coined by his brother, possessed a delicacy which set it apart from the theatrical bras and panties created for Frederick's of Hollywood.

Inside his costume alcove, folded on shelves or swinging from quilted hangers, were scores of exquisite skivvies, in every size imaginable.

Gabe honestly believed that reality comprised the growing requests for intimate glamour photos. Jenn, however, insisted that more was less. Ankle-length nightgowns, she avowed, were much more provocative than naughty costumes. And panty hose were much more comfortable than a garter belt.

"Forget garter belts," he had said, trying to think of a way to explain in words she'd understand. "The plainest woman can look sexy if she strikes the right pose, assumes the right attitude."

"Are you saying *I'm* not sexy?" Without waiting for an answer, Jenn had flounced from the studio.

"Mr. Quinn? Gabe?"

"Sorry, Anne. Are you ready? Shall we get started?"

"Yes. I guess so. I just want to get this over with. The sooner we start, the sooner we'll finish."

Adjusting his array of lights, Gabe wondered if he should seat Anne on top of the antique couch he had discovered at a garage sale. Then inspiration struck.

Denver. Not the city. John.

Gabe's usual choices—Elvis or the Stones, Whitney Houston or Beyoncé—wouldn't do the trick. But there was an old John Denver album on his shelf, wedged alphabetically between the Carpenters and Bob Dylan.

All at once, the lovely poetry that was "Annie's Song"

filled the studio. Anne McFadden's eyes assumed a dreamy expression. Instinctively, her body relaxed.

Bless John Denver, thought Gabe, looking through the lens of his camera.

Chapter Three

"Rocky Mountain hiiiigh . . . Colorado."

Hallie harmonized with her air conditioner. Well, to be perfectly honest, the air conditioner was a mite inharmonious, causing Alice W. O'Brien's voice to sound off-key. Not that Alice W. could carry a tune on the best of nights. In fact, she often lip-synched Christmas carols.

If she wanted music to drown out the loud pitter-patter of her heart, why not adjust her radio's dial? Right now it was set on an all-news station. But all they ever talked about was the heat wave, and Hallie need only glance through her window to see that the lush green golf course, burned by the sun, had turned as colorless as the fingers that clutched her paintbrush.

In any case, it was almost dawn and music from her radio might disturb the sweet retired couple who shared the other half of her duplex.

The air conditioner issued forth one last hum, then a weak whir, then nothing. It had finally surrendered to the omnivorous humidity that covered Bayside—and Hallie—like a soaking wet electric blanket.

She considered shedding her cutoffs and raggedy, sleeveless T-shirt, but she hadn't found the perfect window drapes yet and an improvised bedsheet curtain might subdue the occasional breeze that a whimsical Mother Nature bestowed upon her city dwellers, probably to give them hope.

It was hopeless. Hallie couldn't sleep. She couldn't drown

out the rapid beat of her heart with an off-key John Denver song. And she couldn't stop painting the images that filled her mind, the reason for the rapid beat of her heart.

"Damn, damn, *damn!*" Her shout pierced the curtain of predawn silence. Even the sweltering neighborhood dogs couldn't summon up enough energy to whine, much less bark.

She slammed her brush onto the palette on top of her workbench, spattering her breasts with paint particles that were one-third tangerine, one-third vermilion, and one-third ivory. Feeling the urge to vent her fury on someone or something, she turned toward the painting she'd titled *Archangel.* Propped against the TV screen, directly in front of her unfinished ballerinas, his eyes seemed to follow her every move.

"What the devil's going on, Gabriel? Why did I paint you? And why am I now painting a . . . a parlor house?"

Gabriel didn't answer, of course, but Hallie knew what Marianne would say. She would say, "You were born in the wrong century, kiddo. Tell it like it is."

"Okay, Marianne. A house filled with . . . with . . . women of ill-repute."

Did Gabriel's mouth twitch at the corners? Did his dark eyes mock?

Hallie swiveled her face toward her easel. The painting clamped to its wooden frame, the painting she'd been working on nonstop, depicted a two-story house. Since there weren't any walls, it looked like a stage set. Upstairs, inside various rooms, women were entertaining male visitors. Oh, they weren't engaged in sex, but their intentions were obvious. For one thing, the girls wore scanty attire, mostly corsets and camisoles. A few sported embroidered drawers, and they all looked as though they had selected their undergarments from a nineteenth-century, X-rated catalogue.

If Hallie painted her dream man because she couldn't find the man of her dreams, did that mean she painted a parlor house because, deep down inside, she wanted to be a woman of easy virtue? Or, deep down inside, did she want to select her undergarments from a nineteenth-century, X-rated catalogue?

Probably the latter. She suspected that if/when she got married, her butt would be stamped MAIDEN by a notary public.

Groggy from lack of sleep, bemused by the heat, frightened by the creative impulses she couldn't control, she marched into her bedroom and retrieved a pair of white undies. Stomping back into the living room, she glanced toward the window. An unseen deity's palette knife had scraped away the sunrise and was now spreading buttery sunshine across a vast loaf of blue sky. Soon the butter would melt. Soon Hallie would melt.

Why had she retrieved her undies? Oh, yeah. Picking up her paintbrush, she printed VESTAL VIRGIN across the cotton with the last of her tangerine-vermilion-ivory paint. Then she draped the undies across one corner of Gabriel's canvas.

"This will give you something else to contemplate," she said, feeling utterly ridiculous. Why didn't she simply turn the painting around so that Gabriel faced the wall?

Maybe she wanted to contemplate him. Like any other red-blooded female, she could fantasize. Even Marianne had confessed that, while bathing, she sometimes pictured Brad Pitt.

"Naked?" Hallie had asked, shocked.

"No. Fully clothed. Of course, naked."

"But what about my brother?"

"He prefers Meg Ryan."

"Neil has a thing for Meg Ryan?"

"Everyone has a thing for someone."

At the time, Hallie had thought Marianne's notion absurd. Not anymore. Too bad Hallie's someone didn't exist.

She brought her attention back to the parlor house painting. It was finished, thank goodness. No, it wasn't. One small bedroom remained unoccupied.

Since she hadn't deliberately created any of the other painted women, she waited for her brain to direct her hand. It didn't. That meant the room was supposed to be unoccupied, right?

Inside her belly, fear coiled like a snake. Because she suddenly realized what or, to be more precise, *who* the subject of her next painting would be. She even knew the woman's name.

Lady Scarlet.

Chapter Four

"No, I don't think your mind is playing tricks on you." Marianne shifted six-week-old Shania from one shoulder to the other. "You simply read your mother's history books when you were little and the memory has resurfaced."

"But the paintings are so real," Hallie said, as she leaned back against a soft, leather, cabernet-colored couch cushion. "Most of the women are young, beautiful, and they come in all tints. White, off-white, saffron, sienna, cinnamon, black."

"That's easy to explain. You've just finished a series of paintings on the Dance Theatre of Harlem."

"Almost finished."

"Whatever."

"But my new paintings depict prostitutes, not dancers."

"Hallie, you said the P-word." Marianne tsked her tongue against the roof of her mouth, then grinned impishly.

"Hush." Hallie nodded toward her niece, who had just entered the family room. Draped across Barbra's shoulders, like a black and orange fur stole, was her calico cat.

"Mama," Barbra said, "Cher, Madonna, Tina, Jeff and me want to watch TV." She reached up to pet the cat's white ruff. "Becky, too."

"Cher, Madonna, Tina, Jeff and I," Marianne corrected. "Is your homework done?"

"Yeah. Except for Tina. She's writing a book report."

"Okay. Your Aunt Hallie and I are talking grown-up stuff, so you can watch in my bedroom. Becky, too," she added, sounding like the Good Witch in *The Wizard of Oz*. "Tina can join you when she's done."

"Yippee. Thanks, Mama."

"Don't touch anything except the remote and don't let Madonna teach Jeff another bad word." Marianne turned her lovely face toward Hallie. "I'll put Shania down for her nap."

"Aunt Hallie," Barbra said. "I made you some chocolate chip cookies. They got a little burnt on the bottom, but they're gooey on top."

"Thanks, sweetie. I'll take a bunch home with me so I can have a midnight snack while I'm painting."

"You paint at midnight? Cool! When I'm grown I'm gonna stay up past twelve every night."

"That's what I vowed when I was seven," Marianne mumbled.

Hallie watched Marianne and Shania and Barbra (and Becky) exit the room. When Marianne returned, Hallie said, "I've been rambling on and on about my problems. What's new with you?"

"Dreams happen. Since Shania's miraculous emergence, Neil lets me skip his social gatherings."

"It wasn't miraculous," Hallie mumbled, playing Marianne's embarrassed zebra again.

"Yes, it was." Strolling over to the fireplace, Marianne reached up past the mantel and ran her finger along the frame of *A Midsummer's Night Dream*, one of Hallie's New York City Ballet paintings.

She was searching for stray dust bunnies, Hallie thought, but there weren't any. Despite five kids and four cats (Flopsy, Mopsy, Cottontail and Becky), Marianne's house was as clean as the proverbial whistle.

"Have I told you how much I liked your bit about auditioning for *American Idol* with 'Baby, the Rain Must Fall'?"

Marianne continued. "Or was it 'Rain, the Baby Must Fall'? In any case, you handled Shania's birth like a pro. You even predicted her gender by singing 'My Girl.' "

"You're goofy."

"I'm grateful."

"If you skip social events, when do you ever get a chance to see my brother? Look, Marianne, I can baby-sit."

"No way! You're busy. Don't you have a gallery opening soon?"

"Yes. But I'm all prepared. Six new canvases, seven if you count my dream man. I've painted one a week since Shania was born. I've even titled some of them. *Hallie's Comet*, *The Homestretch*, and I've seriously considered calling my third canvas *Sinatra's Melody*."

"How come?"

"Private joke."

"I love private jokes," Marianne said, sliding gracefully into an overstuffed armchair.

"That's why the lady is a tramp," Hallie sang off-key. "Remember? It was one of Frank Sinatra's biggest hits."

"I don't get it."

Leaning forward, Hallie scrutinized the knee patch on her faded jeans. "My painted lady has blue-black hair and her face is sienna. My little girl has café au lait skin, more milk than coffee, and red curls, the color of overripe strawberries. Yet, there's a definite resemblance. I think the child might be Lady Scarlet's daughter, which would explain why Scarlet took up the profession, so to speak."

"Hallie, you tiptoe round a subject like Sylvester stalking Tweety Bird."

"I do not."

"Yes, you do. Who's Lady Scarlet?"

"A parlor girl from the late 1890s or early 1900s."

"Oh, I get it. That's why the lady is a tramp. Cute." Rising from her chair, Marianne searched through a stack of magazines and catalogues fanned across the coffee table, then selected Victoria's Secret. Opening to a page at random, she said, "Does your painted lady resemble any of these models?"

"Not even close." Conjuring up a naked Brad Pitt, Hallie didn't bother asking why her sister-in-law subscribed to an underwear catalogue. "The child wears a blue wool dress, black stockings, and high-button shoes. Lady Scarlet wears a drab brown skirt and a white blouse, secured at the neckline by a cameo brooch."

"Then how do you know she's a parlor girl?"

"Lady Scarlet and the child are both primly seated on the edge of a horsehair fainting couch and—"

"Wait a sec, Hallie. What's a fainting couch?"

"A sofa shaped like an upside-down L. I looked it up in my antique furniture book."

"That still doesn't prove anything."

Hallie felt her cheeks bake. "Lady Scarlet and the child are both seated beneath an ornately framed picture of a buxom nude woman."

"*You* painted a nude?"

"No. I painted a painting of a nude. And that same couch and picture appear in my second canvas. I think the room is the downstairs sitting room. The furnishings also include plush chairs, an étagère with a petticoat mirror on the bottom, and an old-fashioned piano."

"*The Homestretch.*" At Hallie's startled stare, Marianne smiled. "I'm not a mind reader. You said one of your paintings was called *The Homestretch*. Is that a private joke, too?"

Hallie shook her curls. "It's the name of the parlor house."

"How do you know?"

"I just do. The same way I know Lady Scarlet's name."

"Describe the other rooms."

"Sit down and stop licking your lips, Marianne. There aren't that many details. From the inside, the Homestretch looks like an ordinary boardinghouse. Upstairs are several tiny bedrooms and a viewing room with a hallway window where men can select their . . . um, dates. The ground floor has two parlors, one the sitting room, plus a dining room and kitchen."

"What about the outside?"

"In front are gardens and shrubbery. The back has a covered walkway that leads to the bathrooms. I guess in those days they were called privies. Since my parlor house didn't include walls, I could see through to the back."

"You've completed six new paintings, right? Are the others more detailed?"

"Yes. But they don't depict the Homestretch or Lady Scarlet or the little girl." Hallie's mouth felt dry. She sipped the raspberry lemonade Marianne had served, now diluted by melted ice cubes. "In my paintings, the streets are bordered by wooden buildings, nestled beneath snow-capped mountains. One painting shows a train, the Midland Terminal Railroad."

"How on earth do you know the name of the railroad?"

"It's lettered on the engine. I wrote it there. With a skinny paintbrush. The question is, why did I do that?"

"Do your buildings have names?"

She nodded. "My fifth canvas depicts several saloons, for instance the Combination Miners Exchange, Last Chance, and Swanee River. For my sixth canvas I've used glossy grays and browns, like a tintype photo. The Homestretch is at the end of the block, but other parlor houses are called Laura Belle's, Nell McClusky's, the Old Homestead, and the Mikado. High above the houses I've painted a comet. It looks right, but it doesn't really belong, Marianne, because a comet orbits around the sun and I don't think you can see it, not unless you've set up a telescope."

"Hallie, call your mother."

"Why?"

"Because your paintings have revealed two clues, three if you count the mountains."

"What clues?"

"The Midland Terminal Railroad and the Combination Miners Exchange. It could be a mining town."

"Good grief, Marianne, do you know how many mining towns sprouted in the last half of the nineteenth century?"

"Do you?"

"Of course not, but there must have been hundreds."

"How many were nestled within snow-capped mountains? The comet might be another clue. Call your mother, Hallie. She's a history teacher and a history buff. What have you got to lose?"

What's left of my sanity, Hallie thought. Would Mom laugh? Or say that her only daughter had bats in her belfry?

She needn't have worried. Mom didn't laugh, nor did she mention bats. Instead, Josie O'Brien expressed genuine enthusiasm at the prospect of solving her only daughter's historical puzzle. "I need a break," she said. "I've been grading an exam on the Civil War. Multiple choice. I gave the kids a bonus question. Who's on the fifty-dollar bill? The choices were Ulysses S. Grant, Robert E. Lee, or Spike Lee. Can you guess how many kids circled Spike Lee?" She sighed. "Okay, darling, I'll scan my computer, then my research books, and get right back to you."

Right back took twenty minutes. It seemed like an eternity. Hallie paced, her motions jerky, as if someone pulled the strings on a marionette. She wished she could borrow Jeff's "curity" blanket. Beneath her dark curls, her scalp prickled.

Was her painted town genuine?

Marianne could be right. If Mom's books contained the information she sought, she might have read about mining towns when she was little and stored the information. Like a squirrel storing nuts for the winter.

Was she going nuts? Mom's books could never explain Gabriel. But she had already justified Gabriel. He was her dream man, plain and simple. No, not plain. Her dream man was undeniably handsome, charismatic, and—

Gabriel didn't exist, Hallie reminded herself, except in her imagination. She could paint him over and over, but if she wanted kids she'd better set her sights on a more realistic knight in shining armor. Neil's friend Ivan, for example. He wasn't Ivanhoe, not even close, but he earned a good living on Wall Street and her biological clock was ticking. In ten years she'd be thirty-seven, then fifty.

Gabriel would never age. Lucky Gabriel.

Ivan wasn't charismatic, not by a long shot. But he was handsome, or he would be if he didn't wear his natural hair like a toupee, and he'd never be out of pocket because he didn't spend money as if it was going out of style. In fact, he banked a goodly portion of his fortune "for a rainy day."

To be fair, Ivan wasn't miserly. He took her to every *Times*-approved Broadway show. They never missed the U.S. Open and had courtside tickets for the Knicks. They ate in good restaurants, and if Ivan was a tad stingy with his gratuities, leaving fifteen percent to the penny, she could always make some excuse, return to the table, and put more money on the tip tray.

Recently, Ivan had suggested she "fish or cut bait." Neil nudged, too. He honestly believed that her pragmatism and Ivan's sensible, matter-of-fact mentality would harmonize. Like peanut butter and jelly, ham and eggs, bagels and cream cheese.

Problem was, Hallie liked peanut butter and mayonnaise, bagels and—

The phone's strident ring interrupted her musings.

"Cripple Creek," said Josie, her voice purring with satisfaction.

"Please give me the name again, Mom."

"Cripple Creek, Colorado. It tangles the tongue a bit, doesn't it? I keep wanting to say Crickle Creek."

"How do you know?"

"The Midland Terminal Railroad. One of my history books shows a sketch from the Denver Public Library's Western Collection. The train crosses a trestle, and in the background there are snow-capped mountains. My book also includes an article from a newspaper, *The Colorado Springs Gazette*, dated the June 6, 1900. Do you want to hear it?"

"Yes, please."

" 'A petition was filed by the Midland Terminal Railroad Company asking the city to remove the disorderly houses from the vicinity of the M-T trestles on Myers Avenue.' That same newspaper printed another story, Hallie, a few months later. 'The Fire and Police Committee of the city council has instructed the Police to notify the denizens of the row to keep their windows closed, their blinds down, their doors shut and not to solicit in the streets.' "

"How long have you had that book, Mom?"

"A few years, I guess. Why?"

"I'm trying to figure out what prompted me to paint my train, saloons, and parlor houses."

"Speaking of parlor houses, I couldn't find anything on your Homestretch. But there was a very famous house called the Old Homestead. Maybe you got them mixed up."

"No, Mom. In one of my paintings, the Old Homestead sits in the middle of the block while the Homestretch is farther down the row. All my houses have discreet signs or engraved plaques, some above the doorbells, some above the doors."

Josie chuckled. "It's a bona fide mystery, darling. If I were you, I'd pick up an airline ticket and visit Colorado."

"I can't, Mom. I spent too much money at a charity auction."

"What did you buy?"

"A tennis racket. It was a celeb sports auction and I got caught up in the bidding. I'm afraid Colorado will have to wait until—"

"Do you want Dad and me to buy you a ticket? An early birthday present?"

"Mom, my birthday's eight months away!"

"Okay, a *very* early birthday present. Didn't you once tell me you'd met a young man from Colorado at one of your art seminars?"

"Yes. Joshua Quinn. His father was Simon Quinn, the artist and slain civil rights activist. Joshua inherited his father's genes. And his dreams. He's an illustrator. Children's books. He takes fairy tale characters and changes them into African-Americans. You've seen the watercolor on my bedroom wall. My black Snow White? That's Joshua's."

"In Africa, where snow is virtually unknown, Snow White is called Flower White." Josie chuckled again. "Do you have Joshua Quinn's phone number?"

"I have it. Josh and I went out for dinner and dancing, but there were no sparks, at least not on my part." From the corner of her eye, Hallie could see Marianne's questioning glare. "Josh gave me his address and phone number and said if I ever needed him . . . Mom, Marianne's about to burst. I'll call you later."

"Okay, darling. One last thing. When that temperance,

teetotaling lady, Carrie Nation, visited Cripple Creek, she called it a foul cesspool, the most lawless and wicked city to be found anywhere. She warned the people of the gold camp that Myers Avenue was luring innocent men and women by the hundreds to death and destruction."

"Death and destruction," Hallie echoed. "I believe I will take you up on your birthday gift. Thanks, Mom."

"You're welcome." In a voice tinged with amusement, Josie sang, "Give my regards to Colorado, remember me to Cripple Creek. Tell all the girls on Myers Avenue, that I will soon be there."

"Creek and there don't rhyme," Hallie said pragmatically.

And yet, Myers Avenue sounded awfully familiar and the mere mention of the name caused an ache that was almost tangible.

I've got the blue devils, she thought, even though she had never used that particular expression before.

Chapter Five

Gabriel Quinn massaged his left knee. The darkroom smelled acrid, almost vinegary, but it was a familiar, comforting smell. The safelight had been turned off and two Tiffany floor lamps radiated a warm, stained-glass glow. Despite the nagging ache in his leg, Gabe wanted to shout with joy.

John McFadden's money would be well spent because John Denver's song had achieved miracles.

Yesterday's film had been processed and Gabe couldn't be more pleased. Anne McFadden's face demonstrated exactly the right amount of dreamy seductiveness. Her expression revealed anticipation rather than lust. Her breasts cleaved above the bandanna while her hips seemed to sway rhythmically. Even the mimetic gestures of her hands seemed to say: "I miss you, Johnny, I want you, Johnny, come home to me."

Fortunately, Gabe had shot one roll with his Nikon then switched to his Hasselblad before Jenn had flounced into the studio and jostled his arm, causing him to turn and accidentally shoot the antique couch.

"I've got to talk to you, Gabe," she had said, her perfect, capped teeth clenched.

Suppressing his own anger at the untimely interruption, he had smiled at Anne and suggested she put on her street clothes.

"Don't look so disappointed," he had said. "You were the one who wanted to get this over with."

"But it was fun," she confessed, sauntering toward the

dressing room, her circlet of flowers askew over one bright baby blue eye.

Gabe watched Anne's grass-skirted rump disappear. Then he turned his face toward Jenn, who was clothed in lime green slacks and a matching cashmere sweater. Her body language exhibited displeasure, disdain, disgust. Were there any other dis-words? Yup. Disciplinary. He was about to be chastised.

"She's a tramp," Jenn said scornfully.

"Who? Anne McFadden? You couldn't be more wrong. She's a lady."

"Is that supposed to be funny, Gabe? *The Lady and the Tramp*? If Walt Disney could hear you, he'd turn over in his grave. Or his freezer. Wasn't Walt frozen? In any case, he'd never shoot pornography."

"Neither would I. Listen, honey, there's a big difference between pornographic and provocative. If you posed, you'd see the diff—"

"Not a chance! You won't add me to your stockpile."

"Stockpile? Jenn, what's happened to you? Before I left on my last assignment, you were so"—he paused, thinking *soft, responsive*—"so tolerant. You hated my war photos but you never criticized. Is it my leg?"

"Daddy says your wound is very patriotic."

"What do you say?"

"I didn't come here to argue."

"Why did you come here? Especially when I've asked you to keep away during my photo sessions."

Momentarily, she appeared contrite. "I'm sorry about that, Gabe, but you have to make a decision. Today. Daddy says to fish or cut bait."

"I'm not a fisherman. I'm not a salesman, either. Oh, I get it. This morning, on the phone, I told your father that I didn't want to sell cameras or shoot pictures of babies, unless they're my own. That's why you're fuming. Daddy sent you here to sweeten the pot. My own store, perhaps a chain of stores." Gabe heaved a deep sigh. "Even if I wanted to sell cameras, shoot family photos, and develop vacation snapshots, I would never let your father subsidize my career."

"Nonsense. It would be a wedding gift."

"Your father can give us a video cam, two video cams, but stores filled with photographic equipment? The answer's no. Did you hear me, Jenn? No!"

Uncrossing her arms, she removed her engagement ring. An overhead light captured the diamond's glitter as she extended her hand toward him, the ring dangling from her fingertips.

"Choose," she said. "Me or your professional obsession."

"You can't be serious."

"I've never been more serious in my life."

"Don't you love me?"

"I loved Gabriel Q, not the man who shoots centerfolds."

He noted her use of the past tense, "loved." When had her love turned sour? During the many operations to reconstruct his knee? During his rehabilitation and the agonizing months of physical therapy? Yes, his wound was patriotic and Jenn was bravely performing her patriotic duty by entering into a loveless marriage.

Or was she?

With sudden insight, he realized that Jenn didn't expect him to accept her daddy's offer. She knew he'd never agree, and his refusal gave her the perfect out, the perfect opportunity to break their engagement.

Simply put, Jennifer Bernadette Dominger Greengart couldn't deal with imperfection. Take her art collection, paintings by Hallie O'Brien, ballerinas who were never out of sync, who never stubbed their toes on a land mine or pierced their legs with shrapnel.

Had he loved Jenn? Or had he loved the reflective pride in her eyes when they attended various social functions given by the American Newspaper Guild and Press Photographers Association? At those events his buddies always called him a lucky son of a gun and compared Jenn to every famous model who'd ever graced a runway or decorated a magazine cover.

Why hadn't he sensed Jenn's reluctance to wed a defective man? Because it had never occurred to him, that's why. The important parts of his body worked. He couldn't run, and if the weather threatened he needed a cane, but he'd known Jenn since high school, when he had played wide receiver and she had cheered from the sidelines. Two years of college photography courses and three years of military photography had provided a technically sound background and his career had been exemplary. Jenn said she preferred to wait until he settled down, then they'd get married. Now he was settled. Now he wanted a wife and children. Now she wanted a man with perfect legs.

"Well, Gabe? I'm waiting."

"Keep the ring, sweetheart," he said. "You deserve a reward for your years of devotion, especially the last couple of years."

"Are you saying we should call off our engagement?"

She sounded too eager. Momentarily, he was tempted to capitulate, just to gauge her reaction, but insincerity had never been his strong suit. He had trouble bluffing at a poker game.

"Here's the deal, Jenn. Pose for one of my boudoir photos, and I'll call off our engagement."

"Go to hell! I wouldn't pose for you if you were the—"

"Last photographer on earth?" Feeling strangely unburdened, he watched her flounce from the studio, the ring still dangling from her fingertips.

Her final flounce, thought Gabe, bringing his attention back to the darkroom. He studied the photo he'd shot when Jenn had jostled his arm, and decided that it was thought-provoking even if it did predominantly consist of inanimate objects. He hadn't had time to focus, but his garage sale couch, shaped like an upside-down L, was clearly etched against a folding screen whose hand-painted design included fierce Chinese dragons. The studio lights had caused shadows to produce interesting patterns.

Now Gabe scrutinized those patterns the same way someone else might examine clouds and change them into a billowy mass of sheep. However, his photo shadows were incongruous. For no apparent reason they formed a woman and a child. Both figures were seated on the antique couch. Although their faces were opaque, the woman's hair was skewered into a topknot while the child's long unruly curls looked as if they'd been combed with an eggbeater.

Lord, he was letting his imagination run wild. Maybe the broken engagement had affected him more than he wanted to admit. Maybe he was hungry. Maybe—

The phone's ring interrupted his justifications. Was Jenn calling to apologize? Should he accept her apology? Gabe reached for the darkroom's extension.

"Hi, Scarecrow," said the familiar voice of his younger brother, Joshua.

The scarecrow nickname had been fondly bestowed upon Gabe when he had given up his crutches and his forward motion had been uncertain, his legs rubbery, just like the famous *Wizard of Oz* character.

"Hi, Beast," Gabe said with a grin. Josh had used his own mirrored image to create the prince in *Beauty and the Beast.*

Jenn had posed for Beauty, Gabe recalled, his grin fading. "What's new, baby brother?"

"Nothing much," Josh said. "I've been working on the illustrations for *Jack and the Beanstalk*, but I can't decide whether to make the giant black or white. My damn dog got captured by the pound again—he keeps digging new holes under the fence—and the love of my life plans to visit Colorado."

"Make the giant white, Beast, and sell the dog. Wait a minute! The love of your life? Hallie O'Brien?"

"None other."

"Hey, that's great. Ever since last year's art seminar, you've refused to consider any woman's subtle, sometimes even unsubtle—"

"Her visit's professional, not personal. Hallie was very upfront about that. She's practically engaged to somebody named Ivan, a friend of her brother's."

"Define practically engaged."

"No ring. No wedding date. She prefers to wait."

Gabe thought about Jenn and resentment began to sprout like a seed from a packet of gall and wormwood plants. "No big deal," he said. "Ms. O'Brien's too old for you."

"What? I'm twenty-six. Hallie's twenty-seven. And isn't that the pot calling the kettle black? You're racing toward the big four-oh. Aren't you and Jenn going to tie the knot soon?"

"Nope. The knot's been severed."

"You're kidding. When?"

"Yesterday afternoon."

"I'm sorry, Gabe."

"Thanks, but I feel relieved."

"Bull!" There was a long pause, then Josh said, "Well, I guess that helps with my next question."

"What question?"

"Where Hallie will stay. My house has one tiny bedroom and Napkin dominates the couch."

"Sell the damn dog."

"I can't. He's my best critic. Besides, I owe Napkin my life. He finally forced me to quit smoking by chewing up all my cigarette packs. I paid good money to this guy who swore he could help any poor slob stop smoking and lose weight through hypnosis, but it didn't work."

"It didn't work on you or your fat mutt?"

"Me. Napkin wouldn't go under. He slobbered, rotated his fat furry rump like a fan dancer, licked his jowls, and hungrily eyed the hypnotherapist's swinging watch, which he probably thought was a silver-plated cookie."

Gabe laughed, then said, "Why can't Ms. O'Brien stay at a hotel? Or a bed-and-breakfast?"

"Because she wants to set up her easel and paint. I thought . . . well, Jenn's house has so many spare rooms and . . . hold the phone. Why can't Hallie stay with you? I hadn't considered that, but you have a nice house with a studio and—"

"One bedroom! Where the bloody hell would I sleep?"

"On the sofa."

"You can't be serious."

"Okay, here's another idea. Hallie can use my bedroom, I'll vacuum dog hairs from my sofa, and you can board Napkin."

"Josh, do you have any idea what a St. Bernard with a voracious appetite would do to my studio? At the very least he'd eat my film, and I don't have a fenced yard so I'd have to walk your slobber-jawed mutt. Correction. He'd walk me. I'd rather board your damn artist."

"Thanks, Scarecrow."

Trapped, thought Gabe, admiring his brother's grit.

Josh said, "May I ask one more favor?"

"If I say no, will you threaten me with Napkin again?"

"Hallie's flight lands around three something, I've got it written down. I have to sit by the phone, a conference call, and I can't postpone the call because it involves my agent, *Beanstalk*'s author, and the publisher. Do you have any photo sessions scheduled for tomorrow?"

"No. The last few months I've been booked solid, so I decided to take next week off. I was planning to surprise Jenn, drive up to Cripple Creek, treat her to a show at the Imperial Hotel. I've already bought tickets and made the reservations. I'm free, Beast, very."

"Would you meet the plane, Gabe? Please? She'll be landing in Denver."

Gabe stifled a sigh. "What does your Ms. O'Brien look like?"

Josh didn't stifle his sigh. "She's beautiful."

"All women are beautiful, Beast. Some are beautiful on the inside. Some, like Jenn, spend big bucks fixing what they consider defects. But, when you come right down to it, every woman is—"

"Beautiful. Yes, I know. Hallie has dark curly hair, dark eyes, black-winged brows, thick lashes, and a figure that would make Cinderella's stepsisters gnash their teeth with envy."

"Will she recognize me? Or should I bring a sign?"

"Bring a sign . . ." Josh paused and Gabe could practically hear his brother's face flush. "I never told her about you," Josh confessed.

"Why?"

"I was trying to impress her. With *me*."

"Okay, Beast. I'll meet your Hallie O'Brien. But you owe me, big time."

"Thanks, Gabe. For starters, I'll cover tomorrow night's dinner tab. Any restaurant you choose, the sky's the limit."

Chapter Six

Peering through her small window, Hallie tried to focus on the sky. Her composure was gone and she was nearing the end of her patience. While she wasn't normally a violent person, she wanted to pummel the elderly woman who sat next to her, the woman who wouldn't stop talking about fatal aviation disasters.

"My name's Amelia Capshaw," the elderly lady had stated during take-off. "I was born in nineteen hundred and thirty-two, named for Amelia Earhart. You've heard of her, haven't you?"

"Yes, ma'am. She was the first woman pilot to solo—"

"When were you born, my dear? No. Don't tell me. Let me guess. Nineteen hundred and sixty-nine, right?"

"No, ma'am. I was born in—"

"What a co-inky-dink! An air collision between a passenger jet and a light plane near Indianapolis killed eighty-three people that very same year."

"Please excuse me . . . rest room." Squeezing past Amelia's plump knees, Hallie had staggered to the back of the plane, entered the claustrophobic-sized bathroom, washed her hands, then studied her reflection. Marianne had trimmed her hair and the dark-brown-almost-black curls looked crisp and shiny. Despite the smudged circles of fatigue, her dark-brown-almost-black eyes were shiny with anticipation.

After contemplating her entire wardrobe, she had chosen a white silk blouse with a short black skirt and a matching jacket whose shoulder pads reminded her of a football player.

Well, maybe not that big. Her expression, however, probably mirrored a fierce competitor. Forget death and destruction. She was determined to solve her Cripple Creek mystery and reach the end zone, even if it meant tackling several ghosts along the way.

Upon her return, fastening her seat belt, she saw that Amelia Capshaw looked like nothing less than a human windup toy.

Sure enough, the irksome woman began by talking about Orville Wright's broken propeller blade, which had caused his plane to drop 150 feet, injuring Wright and killing his passenger. Then the pesky Amelia recounted, in detail, the wreck of the 1925 dirigible, *Shenandoah*, followed by the 1937 *Hindenburg* fire. Before Hallie could object, Amelia swiftly enumerated the 1975 Kennedy Airport jet crash, the 1978 San Diego midair collision, and the U.S. amateur boxing team's demise.

"I'll never forget the date, my dear. March fourteenth, nineteen hundred and eighty. It happened over Poland."

She finished, at least temporarily, with the movie *Alive*, including a detailed account of the plane crash. This time a soccer team, rather than a boxing team, was the object of her demented glee.

"They ate dead people," she said, "and they didn't cook 'em first. I wonder if we're going to be fed. I'm hungry. Are you hungry, my dear?"

"No, ma'am, not anymore."

"Delta crashed at the Dallas/Fort Worth Airport, killing one hundred and thirty-three people. The Delta pilot tried to land in a violent thunderstorm. Oh, my goodness gracious." Amelia leaned sideways and stared out through Hallie's window. "Do I see thunder and lightning?"

"I don't think so."

"Yes indeedy, thunder and lightning," Amelia said, her voice smug. Then she continued to chatter away, like a portentous magpie, narrating every terrible accident she could remember. For an old lady, her memory was extremely accurate, especially when it came to the number of people killed.

She halted momentarily to nibble peanuts. At the same time, she slurped a Scotch and Diet Pepsi.

Peering at Colorado's seemingly peaceful sky, Hallie clutched her tapestry handbag and seriously considered bopping the pesky magpie. It was tempting.

Amelia said, "Alaska. Nineteen hundred and seventy-one. The worst single plane disaster . . ." Her voice trailed off as she shut her eyes and began to snooze.

We're approaching Denver, Hallie thought wryly, *and my prophet of doom finally decides to take a nap, bless her heart.*

The sudden silence was almost mind-boggling. Hallie dug through her handbag and removed several Polaroid snapshots. They depicted her paintings:

Archangel.

The Homestretch.

Sinatra's Melody.

The Terminal Express.

Belly Up to the Bar, Boys.

A Hot Time in the Old Town.

And her favorite, *Hallie's Comet.*

Neil would deliver all seven paintings to the gallery, but she fully intended to be back for her new exhibit's opening night. The return date on her birthday ticket was one week from today, which should give her plenty of time. How long did it take to research an old mining town? Especially when, according to Josh, Cripple Creek was almost within spitting distance of Woodland Park.

Along with her two suitcases, she had brought a portable easel, her pinewood paint box, and three primed canvases.

She knew that her creative compulsion still burned like a raging forest fire.

Last night Marianne had cooked dinner for the entire O'Brien clan. Even Neil had turned off his computer and joined the party. Josie was still amused by her daughter's paranormal pictorializations. Hallie's father, the epitome of the absentminded professor, had insisted that most musicians nurtured a paradoxical muse, so why not painters? Marianne continued to hold the belief that Hallie had perused Josie's history books, while practical Neil had loaned his sister the Polaroid.

"Take some snapshots of your paintings," he had suggested, "and compare them to Cripple Creek landmarks. By the way, Ivan says to tell you he has fourth-row tickets for that new Broadway musical, the one the critics are raving about. And," Neil had added, nudging her with an elbow, "the firm just hired a young receptionist with legs up to her chin. She's a bit giggly for my taste, and probably Ivan's, but she idolizes him. Every morning she brings him a skim milk latte and two fresh bran muffins. If the legs don't get him, the bran muffins will, so you might consider sending him a couple of postcards."

"I'll only be gone a week, Neil."

"Call. Or e-mail. You can do that, can't you?"

After hugs and kisses, Hallie had returned to her apartment, carefully aimed Neil's Polaroid, stuffed the results inside her handbag, then packed. Subduing the impulse to start a new painting, she had tried, without much success, to sleep. Unless a change of scenery curtailed her paradoxical muse, tonight she'd itch to curl her fingers around a paintbrush.

"One of the worst commercial disasters took place in nineteen hundred and fifty-six when Trans World and United crashed into the Grand Canyon," Amelia continued, as if she'd never dozed off. "Ike was our president. I voted for him, would have voted for him twice. You're so young, my dear. Have you ever heard of Dwight D. Eisenhower?"

"Yes, ma'am. My mother's a history—"

"When Lyndon Johnson was president—I didn't vote for *him*—there was a midair collision over Danbury."

Approximately thirty-seven minutes later, Hallie sped down the exit ramp, her beige suede boots stepping on toes, her voice murmuring, "Sorry, excuse me, sorry, excuse me." For all she knew, Amelia was still detailing disasters.

Speaking of disasters, the airport looked like a beehive about to burst. Why were there so many people at Denver International Airport on a Monday afternoon?

Looking around, she saw Denver Broncos team members greeting multiple fans. If she knew squat about golf, she knew more than she wanted to know about football. When it came to the NFL, Marianne was a fanatic. Apparently, the Broncos had played a Sunday night away game. Apparently, they'd won. How would she ever find Joshua Quinn in this sea of happy, expectant faces?

Maybe the best plan was to wait until the Broncos headed for the airport exits and pray that Josh didn't get trampled by all those humongous cowboy boots.

She should have known. Victorious football players didn't head for exits. Instead, they joked with the crowd and signed autographs.

Okay. She'd have Josh paged.

Trying to maneuver through the crowd was more difficult than driving the wrong way down a busy one-way street, but she finally managed to reach a service phone. Panting, she leaned against the wall.

Then she saw the poster with its large red letters:

HALLIE O'BRIEN

Clever Josh. Except it wasn't clever Josh. The piece of cardboard was held aloft by a total stranger. Except he wasn't a total stranger.

He was her Archangel.

She shook her head, trying to clear her vision. But her vision wasn't out of focus. There he stood. Gabriel. His hair was dark, long, combed back from his face, emphasizing, no, *dramatizing* those soulful eyes.

Her portrait had stopped at Gabriel's waist. However, she could start a brand-new painting, working from the waist down. Because this man who resembled Gabriel had lean hips, a flat belly, and legs that strained the seams of his faded jeans, as if he'd spent hours, days, months with the latest exercise equipment.

He was tall, perhaps six-three. Turning slightly, his gaze traveled above the crowd, and, for the first time in her life, Hallie felt a savage, almost animalistic impulse to rush forward and rip a man's clothes off.

Why not do it? Everybody else was watching the Broncos. No, they weren't. A few women were casting admiring glances toward *her* Archangel.

An almost overwhelming jealousy caused her to stumble forward.

Dismayed, she dropped her purse, raised both hands to her face, and pressed her fingers against her scorched cheeks. She had lost what little remained of her mind. Because this man wasn't her anything. She was bemused by Amelia's incessant chatter. She was dizzy from the press of people, lack of sleep, hunger, perhaps even fear that her pending search for answers would simply propel her into a maze of incomprehensible questions.

Despite every rationalization, she wanted to fall into this total stranger's arms.

Awkwardly bending down and retrieving her handbag, then walking forward again, she said, "Gabriel?"

"Yes?"

"Gabriel?" Even to her own ears, her voice sounded far away, as if she'd left it inside the plane.

"Yes?" His gaze traveled downward until his eyes caught and held her stunned, disoriented stare. "Hallie?"

"You know me," she whispered.

The airport spun in ever-widening circles and the sea of faces blurred. With the soft mew of a confused kitten, Hallie pitched forward and fell into her Archangel's outstretched arms.

Chapter Seven

Hallie blinked open her eyes. She was entwined by strong arms, one beneath her legs, one cradling the small of her back.

In the distance football players were still signing autographs, so she'd only blacked out momentarily. As her gaze darted left and right, up and down, she saw that her Archangel's cardboard sign now decorated the airport's floor. A sneaker's imprint had almost obliterated the HAL in HALLIE, and a spiked heel had pierced the O in O'BRIEN.

"It looks like a target's bull's-eye," she murmured.

"What looks like a bull's-eye, honey?"

"Your sign." She raised her lashes and focused on his face. "The 'O' in O'Brien."

"Oh." His chiseled features relaxed. Then his arms tightened. "Why did you faint?"

"How did you know I was me?" she countered.

"Josh described you perfectly. Approximately five-five, he said, with hair the color of polished onyx, eyes the color of semisweet chocolate, and a figure that would make Cinderella's stepsisters . . ." He paused, his gaze traveling from her face to her collarbone. "And a heart-shaped locket."

She had a feeling the locket had been an inspirational adlib, halting his highfalutin gab. She also had a feeling that Josh hadn't gone into quite so much detail.

But then, Josh was an author, so maybe he had.

"This was a gift from my great-granny to my mom," she

said, fingering the locket. "Mom gave it to me on my twenty-first birth . . . please put me down."

"First, tell me why you fainted."

"Aviation disaster overload," she half-fibbed. Then, ignoring his quizzical stare, she said, "Who *are* you?"

"I thought you knew my name."

"Gabriel."

"That's right," he agreed.

Her Archangel sounded as if he were humoring a small child, she thought, as annoyance battled confusion.

"Gabriel Quinn," he added.

"Quinn," she echoed.

"My friends call me Gabe. I'm Joshua's brother."

"Joshua's brother?"

"Yup. Josh couldn't meet your plane so he—"

"Where did you get the name Gabriel?"

"My family has this thing for biblical names. What about Hallie?"

"My father's a music buff. Hallie's the mangled version of Alice."

"Cooper?"

"No."

"There's another famous singer named Alice?"

"I thought we were talking about *your* name."

"Gabe's the shortened version of—"

"Gabriel." Hallie shook her head. "I don't believe it."

"I could probably dig up my birth certificate."

She felt her cheeks scorch again. "It's just that I painted a man who looks like you and his name's Gabriel and . . ." She swallowed the rest of her explanation. He might think she was nuts. So what? He already thought she was nuts.

Was she nuts? Now that her emotions had stopped churning like a Jacuzzi, she had time to study his features, especially since his face was so close to hers. There were many differences between her Archangel and Gabriel Quinn. For instance, Gabriel Quinn's eyes were a gray-jade while her dream man's eyes were pure umber. She could picture the tube of paint. Umber.

"They say everybody has a double," Gabe Quinn stated with a slight shrug of his broad shoulders. "Some people even say I look like Mel Gibson."

"Right. Your mouth, uh, smile." She took a deep breath. "Mr. Quinn," she said somewhat desperately, "won't you please, please put me down?"

"Sure. But only if you call me Gabe."

"Yes. Okay. That's a good idea. I prefer Gabe."

"To what?"

"Gabriel."

As he placed her on the ground, she tottered, then quickly regained her balance. "When someone steps off a ship, they've lost their sea legs," she said, hoping he'd believe her brief fainting spell was due to turbulence, which in a sense it was. "What about someone who steps off an airplane?"

"I guess they've lost their sky legs." Retrieving the discarded name poster, he tossed it into a nearby trash can.

Not me, she thought. *I'm walking on air. I've met my dream man and I should be soaring through space rather than wobbling about like some bullyragged jellyfish.*

Bullyragged jellyfish? Where on earth did that come from? First blue devils, now bullyragged jellyfish. What next?

"Do you feel faint again?" Gabe asked, his voice concerned.

She shook her head, then began to stride forward, her feet decisive, like a New Yorker determined to cross the street before the light changed. Marianne had once told Hallie that the person who timed Manhattan's stoplights had a weird sense of humor, perhaps even a death wish.

"Whoa," Gabe said. "Slow down."

Turning, she watched him walk toward her, his gait somewhat choppy. Her dream man limped. No big deal.

She had a sudden thought. Her Archangel portrait stopped at Gabriel's waist. If she had painted his entire body, would he have sported a game leg?

Ridiculous! She was letting her imagination run wild. In any case, she couldn't probe her theory and try another dream man painting because it would look like Gabe Quinn rather than Gabriel Question-mark.

Was Gabe Quinn's beauty skin-deep? Granted, each sight of his sculpted form caused a series of delicious shivers to crisscross her nape. But she was affected by structural perfection. After all, she was an artist.

Structural perfection? In her mind's eye, she could see Marianne. "Tell it like it is," Marianne would say. "You crave to unbutton that starched white shirt, yank it free from those butt-tight jeans, and finger paint that flawless torso. Now, let's talk about his waist, hips and legs."

"Let's not!" Hallie exclaimed.

"Let's not what?"

"Um, waste time. I was contemplating, um, something to eat . . . a pastrami sandwich."

Gabe's laugh was contagious. The sound caused people around them to glance their way, then flash toothy Cheshire cat grins. Hallie didn't get the joke, was immune to his laugh, and felt out of sync.

"What's so funny?" she asked, fingering her locket.

"This is Colorado. As far as we're concerned, pastrami is the name of the football quarterback who, years ago, played for the Houston Oilers. Maybe you should contemplate a buffalo burger."

"New York has Buffalo Bills," she retorted, darting a

glance toward the few remaining Denver Broncos. "And Giants. And at least three delis in my neighborhood serve hot pastrami on seeded rye. They also serve boiled tongue."

Gabe ran his tongue along his lower lip, as if making sure it had survived her diatribe. "Seriously, Hallie," he said, "would you like a sandwich? It's a long ride to Colorado Springs."

"Colorado Springs? I thought Josh lived in Woodland Park."

"He does." Gabe gestured toward a lounge. "How about something to drink? A brandy might settle those sky legs."

"No, thanks. I really should retrieve my luggage. Where do you live, Gabe?" she asked conversationally, striding forward again, although this time she adjusted her gait to his.

"Didn't Josh call last night?" he asked. He looked startled.

"I got home late last night, from a family dinner, and never bothered to check my answering machine. Why would Josh call?"

Halting, Gabe stared down at her. Then he absently tucked a stray curl behind her ear. "I live in Colorado Springs," he said, "not far from Woodland Park, not far from Josh, and . . ." He paused, as if he were about to attempt the "rockets'–red–glare" high notes in "The Star-Spangled Banner."

"And you're going to be my roommate," he finished, grasping her elbow and guiding her onto the automatic walkway.

"Your roommate," she repeated, and felt her eyes widen.

"That's right. You'll use my bedroom and I'll sleep on the couch."

She opened her mouth to object. Before she could, he said, "I lease a two-story house, Hallie. From the outside it looks like a top hat. The crown includes a spacious bedroom and bath and a redwood deck that can't be seen from the front. On the bottom floor there's a family room, a second bathroom, a darkroom, dressing rooms, kitchenette, and I've knocked out some walls to make a studio."

"Studio," she parroted, her mind still trying to assimilate the change of plans. "Did you say darkroom? As in . . . darkroom? You're a photographer!" she said triumphantly, as though she had just solved a "Murder, She Wrote" rerun before the third commercial.

"I'm what's called a boudoir photographer," he said. "I shoot intimate glamour portraits. Do you understand?"

"Of course. I'm not some featherbrained mooncalf."

Gabe smiled at her expressive words, but Hallie felt a vise of fear grip her heart.

Add featherbrained mooncalf to blue devils and bullyragged jellyfish, she thought. *Then try to figure out why you've written a new dictionary inside your head.*

She knew full well what those six words meant—blue devils for sorrow, bullyragged jellyfish for unbalanced coward, featherbrained mooncalf for idiot—but she didn't know why she was suddenly chitchatting in what Marianne might call "obsolete speak."

Although she sometimes took a break from her everyday, stress-related world by devouring Marianne's historical romance novels, she remembered characters, not their dialogue. What about historical movies? *The Last of the Mohicans. Glory.* Did an Indian or Union soldier shout "Bullyragged jellyfish!" while scalping or shooting his adversary?

"I don't think so." Noting Gabe's puzzled expression, she quickly added, "I don't think I should stay with you."

"Why not?"

"I'd be imposing."

"Define imposing."

"Sometimes, especially late at night, I paint."

"When the sun goes down, I hibernate. Nothing disturbs

me. For the next few nights I'll hibernate in the family room. There's a fairly large alcove where I keep costumes and props, just off the studio. It would be a perfect place for you to paint," he urged. "You can't stay with my brother, Hallie. For one thing, he has a fat St. Bernard named Napkin, the size of a small pony."

"Napkin?"

"Josh christened him Napkin because, even as a puppy, he licked crumbs from the table, not to mention faces. In any case, Napkin would chew up your paintbrushes while you slipped into blissful slumber."

I haven't enjoyed much blissful slumber lately, she thought.

"I don't own an alarm clock," Gabe said, "because I have a bird feeder and the magpies tend to wake me at sunrise. They'll wake you, too. If you get up and prepare fresh coffee, we'll call it even."

"I've never developed a taste for coffee, but I suppose I can follow the directions on the can. How hard could it be to cook coffee?"

"Brew, Hallie. One brews coffee."

"Will you let me pay for food and lodging? If not, forget—"

"I've got a much better idea. I want to increase my business by marketing a new portfolio, so you can be my model."

She had a feeling he had just improvised the model-portfolio bit. "Clothed or unclothed?" she snipped.

"Clothed. My brother says you plan to explore Cripple Creek. I'd like to shoot some photos of old landmarks with you dressed in authentic garb. The Mollie Kathleen gold mine, the Imperial Hotel, the Old Homestead—"

"The Old Homestead?"

"Yup. It was a famous—"

"Parlor house."

"You've heard of the Old Homestead?"

It's in one of my paintings, she thought.

Aloud, she said, "I read up on Cripple Creek before I left New York. My mother's a history teacher. She mentioned the Old Homestead."

There! She hadn't lied. Her mom *had* talked about the famous parlor house.

"A photo shoot sounds like fun," she added, hoping he wouldn't ask her why she wanted to explore the mining town.

"Unfortunately," Gabe said wryly, "there aren't very many old landmarks still left intact."

"What do you mean?"

"Didn't Josh tell you? There are slot machines everywhere. Gambling's legal in Cripple Creek."

Hallie felt as if she'd been punched in the stomach. Denver International Airport receded while images whirled.

The inside of a saloon.

A poker table.

Seated at a table were five men and a heavy woman shaped like a box. The woman's corset thrust her abundant breasts above her bodice. Had she not worn a corset, her breasts would have sagged to her waistline.

"I'll throw in my gramophone," said one of the men, his beard not quite hiding his scowl, "if you bet your Knickers." He pointed to a young girl who stood nearby.

The boxy woman looked down at her cards. "Your gramophone's worth thirty dollars. My Knickers is worth much more. Throw in your horse."

The young girl gasped. "Don't bet your horse, Gabriel," she said. "You need your horse."

Ignoring her plea, the bearded man nodded, his dark hair haloed by clouds of cigar smoke.

"It's a deal, madam," he said.

"How's that for a deal?" Gabe said.

"Huh?" Reaching out blindly, Hallie clutched his muscle-corded arm.

"You model for me and . . . honey, are you all right?"

"Yes. Of course I'm all right. Why wouldn't I be all right?" She shook her head, then flexed her arms and legs, as if she played put-your-whole-self-in-and-shake-it-all-about. "I suddenly felt light-headed, that's all."

Gabe chuckled. "It's the altitude. Most people feel light-headed when they first hit Colorado. We're so high up, the mountains tickle God's feet."

Chapter Eight

We're so high up, the mountains tickle God's feet.

Gabe hadn't exaggerated, Hallie thought, as she gazed with awe at the distant mountain peaks, already sprinkled on top with early snowfall, looking like a chocolate pistachio sundae sprinkled with coconut. Lord, she was starving.

As if he'd read her mind, or heard her tummy growl, Gabe downshifted.

"There's a Red Lobster not far from this exit," he said. "Josh and I reckoned you'd be starving, so my brother suggested we meet in Colorado Springs, around five. According to my dashboard clock, it's 5:10. We didn't know what kind of food you like, but—"

"Lobster's great. I love all seafood. Unless I eat at my mom's or my sister-in-law's, I'll order Chinese takeout." She fiddled with her seat belt. "Five ten? I dozed for an hour and a half? Holy Moses!"

This time her newest obsolete speak, "Holy Moses," didn't shock her mind. Or body. After all, her epigrammatic catchwords had something to do with her strange paintings and she planned to solve that particular paradox.

"I'm going to face that Irish bull head-on," she stated, her voice resolute.

"Irish bull?" Parking his Chevy Blazer, Gabe slanted her a puzzled glance.

"Isn't that your brother? Standing by the restaurant door?

Sure it is. The Huck Finn grin and dreadlocks are dead give-aways."

Unsnapping her seat belt, Hallie found the ground with her boots, then raced toward Josh and gave him a bone-crushing hug.

"Damn," he exclaimed, holding her at arm's length. "You're even more beautiful than I remembered."

"Don't be silly." She felt her cheeks bake. "I've seen your illustrations for *Beauty and the Beast.* Now *there's* a beauty."

"Only on the outside," Gabe mumbled. He couldn't quite believe the acute stab of jealousy he'd experienced when Hallie hugged his brother. He had known her a little over three hours, and yet he felt as if he'd known her forever. Or at least met her before. What a cliché. If he wasn't careful, he'd tell her he was a Leo and ask for her sign. On second thought, he didn't need to ask. She'd been born in May. "When's your birthday, Hallie?"

"May eighteenth, Gabe. Why?"

Josh chuckled. "My brother thinks you're too old for me."

"I'm not too old for any man. I'm not too young, either."

Hallie realized her retort was irrational. But she also realized that her dream man would adopt a hands-off policy. His brother had already staked a claim. Well, hunky-dory! Her first reaction at the airport, her impulse to rip Gabriel's clothes from his body, scared her. Gabe's clothes, not Gabriel's clothes. She'd have to remember to keep Gabe and Gabriel separate.

"What did you mean by Irish bull?" Gabe whispered, escorting her inside the restaurant.

I was talking obsolete speak, she thought, adding "hunky-dory" to her list. "My father's Irish," she whispered back, the first clarification that came to mind.

"Okay, but—"

"Hush. Josh might think we're exchanging intimate secrets."

"That comes later, along with dessert and coffee."

"I don't drink coffee."

"You might try some tonight. If you add Baileys *Irish* Cream, it sweetens the taste."

"What are you two whispering about?" Josh asked, as a hostess led them to their table.

"Coffee," Gabe said. "Hallie's never developed a taste for the bitter brew so I suggested she add a liqueur."

"She can have anything her little heart desires," Josh said.

No, she can't, Hallie thought, *because her little heart desires Gabe.*

"What a flapdoodle," she blurted.

"A flap-what?" Josh arched one eyebrow.

"Doodle," said Gabe. "Hallie has all kinds of quaint expressions you wouldn't expect from a sophisticated New Yorker. Didn't you notice when you met her at the art seminar?"

"Not really." Josh picked up his menu. "I'll order for all of us. Shrimp cocktails and stuffed mushrooms to start, then Maine lobsters. How does that sound?"

"Expensive," Hallie murmured.

"Don't fret, sweetheart. During this afternoon's conference call, we all decided to collaborate on another project, *The Ugly Duckling*. My publisher's advance payment will be generous and I'm already picturing a black swan."

Gabe and Josh exchanged a high five across the table.

"Good for you, Beast," Gabe said. "Damn, we have two celebrities present. Joshua Quinn and Hallie O'Brien."

"Three," said Josh. "Don't exclude yourself, Scarecrow."

While the brothers explained their nicknames, Hallie's mind raced. What had Josh meant by three celebrities? A boudoir photographer wasn't a celebrity, unless he hobnobbed with the rich and famous. Did Britney Spears and Cher, both of whom favored scanty underwear and belly buttons, schedule photo sessions?

Before she could ask about celebs and their belly buttons, the waitress sidled table-side. Josh captured her attention completely. He had the Quinn charm: a subtle, flirtatious energy. He was also undeniably attractive, with his hazel eyes and mischievous smile. Josh was an open book while his brother possessed a dark, brooding, almost Gothic quality. With Gabe, you'd want to sneak an early peek at the last chapter, only to discover that the last chapter was missing. While the idea itself was thought-provoking, right now she had more than enough mystery in her life. She preferred to read the pages where the hero rescued the heroine from the castle's uppermost parapet and they lived happily ever after.

The shrimp cocktail was delicious. So were the stuffed mushrooms, dripping with melted cheese. Two bites into her Caesar salad and she felt stuffed. She shouldn't have let Josh order the lobster. Too late. Their waitress, Gretchen, was presenting Hallie's red crustacean with a flourish. It had large claws, a curled-up belly, and a *head.* The only lobster she'd ever eaten was lobster thermidor, where the meat was mixed into a rich wine sauce then stuffed into its shell and browned. The only whole lobster she'd ever seen was in Disney's *The Little Mermaid.* Her stomach lurched, and she didn't care if her lobster came from Maine or Minneapolis or the moon. Its dead, beady, stalked eyes stared accusingly.

Gabe's dark eyes stared compassionately. He seemed to be on the same wavelength, thank goodness.

"Gretchen," he said, "would you be kind enough to tote our lobsters back into the kitchen, remove their heads, then place their remains in three to-go boxes? Our lovely guest just arrived from New York and she's two hours ahead of us. Not quite jet-lagged, but close."

"Of course, sir. May I bring you coffee? Dessert? Our key lime pie is featured tonight."

"That sounds great. Hallie?"

"No, thank you. Hot tea would be nice."

"Two slices of pie," said Gretchen, "two coffees, one hot tea, and three Styrofoam coffins for the lobsters."

Gabe's nod and smile promised a very generous gratuity. Hallie wanted to hug him. She wanted to hug Gretchen. She wanted to hug Josh, who was looking perplexed yet had the good sense to remain silent.

I'm on emotional overload, she thought, as Gretchen returned with the beverages and dessert. The desire to hug had become a desire to sniffle, and Hallie felt dewy-eyed. Reaching into her purse for a packet of tissues, her fingers brushed against the Polaroid snapshots.

Glancing down, she saw *The Homestretch*.

Gabe, Josh, Gretchen, tables, chairs, fish plaques, and a billboard that announced the fresh catch of the day, all receded while new images whirled.

The inside of a small bedroom.

A dragon-decorated screen.

A spool bed.

A leather-thonged chest.

A dressing table cluttered with bottles labeled Creme de Marshmallows, Princess Hair Restorer, Milk of Cucumber and Dr. Hammond's Nerve and Brain Tablets.

Seated at the dressing table was a beautiful woman, her hair skewered into a topknot, crimped curls hugging her face.

Near her stood a child. The child wore underwear, loose-fitting white panties gathered at the knees.

"I cook coffee best," the child bragged.

"I cook coffee best," Hallie bragged, her voice young and sluggish. "It's easy. I stand on a chair, fill a big pot with boiled water and roasted mocha grounds, add the white of an egg, or a few shavings of isinglass, or a dried bit of fish skin. Ten minutes later the coffee's ready. Cook lets me do it while she starts the custards and all-day roasts."

"Hallie!" Gabe's voice reflected his alarm. "Hallie, wake up!"

"Huh?" She felt her heart hammer. "Why are you looking at me like that? Holy Moses, Gabriel, what did I say?"

Chapter Nine

"I've never cooked . . . brewed coffee, Gabe, but I don't believe one adds dried fish skin, or wet fish skin, or any other kind of epidermis."

Gabe watched Hallie march up and down his family room as if she were a soldier on parade. A barefoot soldier. After removing her suit jacket and boots, she had performed an adorable snake-like hula, her hands beneath her skirt. Finally, with a sigh of relief, she had shed her panty hose.

"Women used to cut off their circulation with corsets and garters," she had grumbled. "Now they glove their legs in panty hose. You'll never find a man binding his legs with elasticized nylon."

"That's right, honey. A man binds his throat with a tie. Why not be honest and call it a hangman's noose?"

"You're not wearing a tie." After stopping to inspect Gabe's open shirt collar, she had resumed her march.

Outside, the wind huffed and puffed like the big bad wolf. Inside, it was warm and cozy. A floor lamp cast its muted glow across one corner of a beige corduroy sofa. Overhead track lighting emphasized white walls decorated with movie posters, an eclectic assortment that included Ray Bolger as *The Wizard of Oz* scarecrow, Sylvester Stallone in *Rocky*, Gregory Peck in *To Kill a Mockingbird*, Whoopi, Oprah and Danny in *The Color Purple*, Daniel Day-Lewis in *The Last of the Mohicans*, Kirk Douglas in *Spartacus*, and Harrison Ford as Indiana Jones.

Directly above the fireplace mantel hung a portrait of

Jenn. The artist had worked from one of Gabriel Q's earlier photographs and Jenn had given the painting to Gabe as a birthday present. For the first time, he noticed that her features were perfectly rendered but her expression was devoid of any true emotion. Passive lips, he thought critically. And blank eyes that brought to mind a goldfish.

The rest of his furnishings were functional—a red-bordered Turkish prayer rug, a polished redwood coffee table, a wall unit with a plethora of electronic equipment, and handcrafted shelves filled with mystery novels and Joshua Quinn– illustrated books.

"Dried fish skin," Hallie repeated for the umpteenth time, bumping into Gabe's rock-hard chest.

"Forget the damn coffee," he said, "and sit down. You look like you're about to—"

"Faint?"

"No. Explode."

"People don't explode."

"They do verbally." Gabe glanced at the portrait above the fireplace. Then his gaze returned to Hallie's face. It revealed an apprehensive vulnerability that tugged at his heart. "I'm sure there's a simple explanation."

"For my cooking lesson or my obsolete speak?"

"Obsolete speak? What do you mean?"

"I'm a New Yorker, Gabe, born and bred. I've never used quaint expressions before. I've never said 'featherbrained mooncalf' or 'Irish bull' or 'Holy Moses' or 'flapdoodle.' And I've never, ever used the phrase 'blue devils.' "

"Blue what?"

"Devils. The blues. I think I've got them now." With a weary sigh, she sank onto a couch cushion. "When will Josh be back? All he said before he took off was 'Napkin.' Then he blew me a kiss and slammed the door."

"He won't be back tonight, Hallie. While you visited the bathroom, he called home and checked his answering machine. There was a message from his next-door neighbor. Napkin likes to tunnel under the fence and saunter off to menace the neighborhood or visit various lady friends. Josh had him neutered but the desire is still there, if not the technology." Gabe waited for Hallie to smile. She didn't. "Anyway," he continued, "the next-door neighbors own this huge black Persian named Eartha Kitt."

"Eartha Kitt," she echoed. "My father would love that."

"Eartha purred her songs," said Gabe, relieved to see Hallie's lips crease upwards and her taut features relax. "Her voice could send shivers up and down your spine."

"My voice generates shivers, too. It sounds like fingernails scratching a chalkboard." She sighed. "Poor Dad. He's into music, big time, and he had such high hopes."

"Yes, I remember. At the airport you said you were named for a singer named Alice somebody or other. Alice W. I'm a music buff like your father, but I still can't fathom what the W—"

"My brother, who was named for Neil Diamond, can't sing either. We're hoping Neil's kids, all christened for various singers, aren't tone-deaf. Don't they fight?"

"Who? Your brother's kids?"

"No. Napkin and Eartha Kitt."

"Yup. They fight like cats and dogs. The neighbors usually lock Napkin in their kitchen until Josh collects him."

"What nice neighbors."

"Three years ago Josh used their cat as his model for *Puss in Boots*. He also used their daughter, a high school senior, for the princess. She had joined a gang, but quit to pose. Josh talked her into applying for a college scholarship. The neighbors were grateful, and charmed by Josh's illustrations.

They've got autographed copies of his book, an original sketch of Eartha as Puss . . ." Gabe swallowed the rest of his words. "Hallie, what's wrong?"

"I'll let my pets go when their wounds heal. President Roosevelt's son has a garter snake. He named it Emily for a skinny aunt."

"Hallie!"

"The Roosevelts have cats and dogs, too," she said, her voice a plea. "And guinea pigs, a black bear, a parrot, ponies, and a kangaroo. They all live inside the White House, though it's not gonna stay white if the Roosevelts' pets mess like mine do. That was a joke, Gabriel. Please laugh. Mama Scarlet made me give my pets away. But you'll let me keep them, won't you?"

Thoroughly alarmed, Gabe sat on the couch and pulled Hallie into his lap. "Honey, wake up!"

"I'm not asleep. Oh, God! I just said something stupid, didn't I?"

"No, not stupid. Baffling. You mentioned Scarlet and—"

"Lady Scarlet?"

"No. Mama Scarlet."

"I knew it! I told Marianne—my sister-in-law—I told her Scarlet was the little g-girl's m-m-mother."

"Aw, don't cry." Gabe pressed her face against his shoulder. "Should I call Josh?"

"No. Please. Josh and I, we're friends, that's all. He wouldn't understand."

"I don't understand," Gabe said, striving to keep his voice soft and comforting.

"But you must."

"Why must I?"

"Because you're Gabriel."

He tilted her chin and stared into her tear-drenched eyes.

"You'd better start at the beginning."

"I painted you. Then I painted her. Lady Scarlet. Well, not really. I mean, she was missing. The room was empty. But it was her room, just like the little girl is her daughter. Then I painted them both, seated on top of a couch shaped like an upside-down L. Then I painted a train and a street, Myers Avenue, and a comet, and I had the blue devils because I knew something *bad* was going to happen."

"To whom? Lady Scarlet?"

"Yes. No. I don't know."

"Is that the reason for your visit? Does Lady Scarlet live in Colorado?"

"Yes. Cripple Creek."

"Does she have a last name?"

"I guess. Doesn't everybody? Why?"

"If we can ferret out her last name, we can call and warn her."

"Gabe, my paintings depict the 1890s."

"Teddy Roosevelt."

"What?"

"You talked about the Roosevelts and their pets. Teddy Roosevelt was president from 1901 to 1909."

"Okay, so I'm off by a few years. Or my little girl's not so little anymore. Or I'm going back and forth and can't control her age."

"Hallie, listen to yourself. You can't control her age? That makes no sense."

"If I can't control my vivid images and my paintings, hopscotching the age of a child makes perfect sense."

"Maybe," he said thoughtfully, "you read *Gone With The Wind* when you were a kid. Maybe you saw the movie."

"Both. But *my* Scarlet is spelled like the color red and she's a parlor girl from Colorado."

"There's got to be a logical explanation."

"There is. I'm stuck inside the Twilight Zone."

"Hush," he soothed. "I'm not in any zone, twilight or otherwise, and you're here with me."

"Am I really? This isn't a dream?"

His reply was a kiss. He had meant it to be a physical reminder, like pinching someone to prove they're awake, but her lips parted and he thrust his tongue inside.

Hallie pressed her body closer to Gabe's. The unpliable expanse of his chest adapted to her breasts and his leg muscles tightened as she sank deeper into the crevice between his thighs. Another portion of his anatomy grew, she could *feel* it grow, and a panicky trepidation blotted out what little remained of her rational mind. With an effort, she stayed motionless. With an even greater effort, she refrained from skidoodling . . . and where the heck did *that* word come from?

The kiss continued. He tasted tangy. In her wildest imagination, she had never thought her dream man's kiss would taste like key lime pie. But then she had never thought a kiss would drain all the strength from her arms. In another moment, she'd release his neck. No. Another second. What was shorter than a second? A trice? How about an instant?

It didn't matter. While she had contemplated less-than-no-time time, her head had landed on the cushion to the right of his knee. The rest of her body spread lackadaisically across his thighs.

Their magical kiss had ended. But that didn't matter, either. Gabe's hands were lightly pressed against her tummy. She had no desire to move, didn't feel embarrassed or shy. His fingers began to rove, creating a coil of heat that traveled from her belly to her legs, and yet his strokes felt *familiar*. So did the unbearable ache in her breasts, beneath her camisole. Her nipples pressed against her blouse. Frightened again, she was tempted to escape from his fingers and rise to her feet.

Suddenly, as if her brain had shifted into reverse, she could hardly wait until he unbuttoned his trousers.

Unbuttoned his trousers? Jeans didn't unbutton. They unzipped, unless they were special Levi's, and Gabe's fly had a zipper. She had felt it. *Gabe's fly had a zipper, and she wore a bra, not a camisole.*

"Wait, please, wait." She struggled to sit up. "I thought you were Gabriel."

"I am Gabriel."

"The other Gabriel."

Gabe disentangled Hallie from his lap. Rising from the couch, he said, "Let's get one thing straight. I'm Gabriel Quinn, not somebody's double. Okay?"

She stood on coltish legs. He watched her retrieve her purse from the coffee table and reach inside. With hands as shaky as her legs, she handed him a packet of photographs.

He flipped through them slowly. "These are your paintings?"

"Yes."

"You've changed your style."

"How do you know my style?"

"I've seen your ballerinas."

She was staring intently at his face, anticipating his reaction, so Gabe tried to remain impassive, especially when he came to the picture of his double. It was flattering, almost too flattering. There were no imperfections. Hallie's rendition didn't show the small scar across his chin, the result of a swift fall to the ground during his Northern Ireland assignment. Hallie's rendition increased his chest by a couple of inches and gave him pecs that would make a heavyweight contender scramble between the ropes. "I give up," the contender would howl. "Let Rocky fight Gabe."

Gabriel, not Gabe. *He* would have to keep them straight.

Had Hallie responded to Gabe's kiss? Or Gabriel's?

Strange to think that Gabe Quinn's rival wasn't his brother, Josh. It wasn't even Hallie's so-called fiancé, Ivan. Gabe's rival was a man who didn't exist. If he did, he'd be hanging up there on the wall, along with the other movie stars.

That thought brought Gabe back to the immediate present and Hallie's expressive eyes. Her gaze still probed his face.

"These are great," he said with genuine enthusiasm. "Your paintings have an old-fashioned playfulness. And yet, in my humble opinion, your painted women could pose for a calendar, or the *Sports Illustrated* swimsuit edition. And your comet is awesome."

"I'm mad as a March hare, right?"

He was tempted to grin at her latest offbeat phrase. "Wrong. I bet it's subliminal."

"Subliminal? My mind is functioning below the threshold of conscious awareness? Like a television commercial?"

"Exactly. You read a book or saw a film and—"

"That's what Marianne says," she interrupted. "Well, duh! Josh might have mentioned you at the art seminar. I don't remember him calling you Gabriel or giving a physical description, but we talked about so many things. When I began to paint my dream man . . ." She paused, her cheeks aflame. "Okay. Let's figure this out, step by step, logically. I was painting ballerinas for my gallery show. I promised the gallery six new canvases. Usually I thrive on pressure, but this time I must have felt stressed. So I took a commercial break. I painted you, probably from something Josh said. Then my subconscious continued directing my brain and I created Lady Scarlet. Gosh, I feel better."

"I'm glad I could help."

"Help? You're a godsend."

She was the godsend, Gabe thought. A godsend was a desirable thing that comes unexpectedly. Hallie had certainly burst into his life unexpectedly . . . just as Jenn had unexpectedly exited.

Was he caught in a rebound vortex?

No. He didn't believe that. His relationship with Jenn had been deteriorating for months. However, he must not forget that his brother had staked the first claim. Even if Hallie didn't reciprocate, Gabe had no right to trespass.

"I can't thank you enough," she said, her voice tremulous.

On tiptoe, she molded her fingers around his neck and gave him a kiss that seared his lips. All his clear reasoning wended its way up the chimney. Like smoke. He was drawn to Hallie, the same way a nail was drawn to a magnet. Or, to use another, more apropos cliché, a moth to a flame.

"Gabriel," she breathed, just before she captured his tongue.

His hands inched her skirt up until he encountered cotton panties that felt like silk. Or did her supple thighs feel like silk? He was so intoxicated by her kiss, he couldn't tell the difference. With a moan, she straddled his hips. Good. Now her face was level with his, and he could give her tongue the attention it deserved. He could also give her curvy rump the attention *it* deserved. He ached to nuzzle her breasts and lick her nipples, but that would come later. Maybe not. As he fondled her buttocks, she let go of his neck and began to sink backwards.

He lowered her to the Turkish prayer rug. Her legs relaxed. Long lashes shaded her cheeks. He couldn't make a coherent decision. Should he taste her sweet breath again? Or should he search out the hidden treasure that lay buried beneath her blouse and bra?

"Gabriel," she breathed. "Oh, Gabriel, I've waited so long. Years and years."

Despite his heart's thunder, Gabe heard her whispered words. This time he knew she was responding to the man in her painting, her perfect man.

He felt a flash of disappointment, then anger. Why not take advantage of her confusion and play her subliminal hero? When he finished, she would concede that reality was more satisfying than dreams.

But that would be too late. He wanted her awake now, aware now, responding to *him*.

"Gabriel, why do you hesitate?" she whimpered. "Is it because I'm pure?"

Gabe sat back on his heels. Pure? Was Hallie a virgin? He recalled her wide-eyed gaze at the airport when he'd mentioned the roommate thing. Yes, she was a virgin, or a very competent actress. No. Jenn acted. Hallie possessed integrity. He didn't know her very well, but he knew that much.

"Honey?" He leaned forward and gently traced the contours of her face. "Honey, wake up."

She blinked open her eyes. "I'm on the floor. Did I faint?"

"You swooned," he said. It wasn't the whole truth, but it was close, and he didn't want to frighten her.

"I've never fainted in my life," she wailed, sitting up. "Today, twice. You must think me a silly goose. There I go again. I've never said 'silly goose' before. I've never even tasted goose, or cooked one's goose, or *brewed* a goose."

"Hush. You're physically and emotionally exhausted, that's all." Rising, he extended his hand and helped her to her feet.

"I remember thanking you and kissing you. Did I swoon from your kiss?"

"Probably," he teased. "I tasted my first real kiss when I was in the fifth grade. It was wet, very wet, and the girl upon whom I bestowed the honor called me a basted frog. In retrospect, I'm sure she meant bastard frog."

Hallie gave him a tight-lipped grin, just before she said, "You have to kiss a lot of basted frogs before you find your prince."

"I've practiced since the fifth grade and my kisses aren't quite so sloppy. I don't think I'm proficient enough to cause swoons, but I'm working on it."

"I think I'll retire."

"From kissing? You're awfully young to retire from—"

"Bed, Gabe. If you don't mind, I'll retire to your bedroom. I'm suddenly so exhausted I can't see straight."

She did look dog-tired, he thought. Circling her waist, he guided her up the staircase, turned right, then entered his bedroom. It smelled of freshly laundered sheets. The moon shone through an overhead skylight, casting a diluted glow across his bureau, desk, and king-sized bed. Hallie headed straight for the bed, sank down upon its mattress, and closed her eyes.

Poor baby. He was tempted to massage her tense shoulders, but she had already turned over onto her side and fallen fast asleep. What about her clothes? Forget it. He had a washer and dryer. If her outfit was dry clean only, they'd deposit it at the cleaners on their way to Cripple Creek. He was anxious to visit Cripple Creek. He had soothed Hallie's fears, at least temporarily, with un–Twilight Zone logic. But he knew, for a fact, that his brother hadn't mentioned him during the art seminar. Furthermore, "subliminal" didn't cover her quirky conversational lapses. Or Gabriel. Who the hell was Gabriel?

There was a definite link between Gabriel, Lady Scarlet,

and Scarlet's daughter. Gabe was a movie buff as well as a music buff. Now he tried to probe his memory for a similar plot, or at least a Gabriel. He'd remember that name since it was his own. Nope. Didn't ring a bell. Yes, it did. There was a 1950-something movie where Clark Gable had played a man named Gabriel. But the heroine wasn't Lady Scarlet. In fact, the only Scarlet Gabe knew of was O'Hara, Scarlett, spelled with two t's at the end.

Could Lady Scarlet be a pseudonym?

If true, she'd be impossible to trace, assuming she'd actually existed. What about her daughter? The daughter didn't even have a name.

Gabe stifled the impulse to snap his fingers. He recalled the photo he had shot when Jenn jostled his arm; the shadow of a woman and child seated on his antique couch. Could the woman be Scarlet? Could the child be little Miss No Name? Come to think of it, that very same couch had appeared in two of Hallie's paintings. Which meant . . . what?

Which meant that he was as mad as a March hare, too. Or that he and Hallie were connected by the past.

Gabe liked to read about the past, but he liked to live for the present. And the future.

I want to establish a future with Hallie O'Brien!

He yearned to blurt the words out loud. He yearned to tell her that the thought of losing her caused an ache far worse than the one he'd felt when the pretty fifth-grader called him a basted frog.

Tomorrow he and Hallie would drive to Cripple Creek. Tomorrow they'd try to unravel the mystery of Scarlet, Gabriel, and the little girl. There had to be a logical explanation.

As he closed the bedroom door, Gabe thought he heard her murmur, "Don't forget to give your Knickers a good night kiss."

Chapter Ten

Hallie awoke with a start. Gabe didn't have a bedroom clock so she couldn't determine the time. The overhead skylight displayed an infinity of stars, haphazardly pinned to a bolt of black velour.

Gabe had left the hallway lit. Clothed in her rumpled skirt and blouse, she navigated the staircase, which led directly to the family room.

Her Archangel slept on the sofa, his dark lashes shading his cheeks. The blanket had slipped and she saw that he didn't wear pajamas, at least not on top. She had expected a mat of fur to dominate the vast expanse of his chest, but it didn't. Pale moonlight, spilling through the windowpanes, revealed sleek, etched muscles. Gabe looked like an ad for an exercise machine, the TV ad where a male model exhibits different parts of his body and hints that viewers could achieve the same result if they invested a few measly dollars a month, plus shipping and handling, satisfaction guaranteed.

Satisfaction. Oh, yes. *Handling.* She wanted to trace those hard muscles until her hand tired of its task. No. Until her lips tired.

Crazy! She was acting crazy again. She had known Gabe less than one day. Well, less than three months, if her dream portrait counted, and yet she honestly felt as if she'd known him for a hundred years.

With a sigh, she tiptoed into the alcove where he had set up her easel. After pressing her thumb against a light switch, she saw that her primed canvases leaned against the wall. Her paint box lay on top of a table, along with various studio props.

Three hours later, a new painting adorned her easel. The painting depicted a bull and matador. In the distance, bleachers and box seats were filled with people, some standing, some sitting, all cheering.

Well . . . almost all.

Highlighted by a cyclone of sunshine that spiraled down from the top of the canvas, one young girl looked stunned. No. Distressed.

She wore a yoke dress, the material falling loosely from the stitched smocking on her chest. Her red hair had been drawn up and back to display her ears, but unruly curls tumbled, willy-nilly, to frame her small, heart-shaped face. Her feet were shod in boots and in her hands she clutched a bonnet.

On their own volition, Hallie's fingers curled tightly around her paintbrush.

As if directed by a master puppeteer, she added a couple of quick strokes.

Now, the girl screamed.

Dropping the paintbrush, Hallie stepped back, away from the painting.

The bull's slick hide glistened. The matador, dressed in black and gold, held a red cape aloft. There were many other scrupulous details, including a dark blue sky that resembled the bunting on an American flag.

Not unlike a swimmer emerging from the depths of a chlorinated pool, Hallie rubbed her eyes. She was vaguely aware that her skirt and blouse were paint-spattered, but she didn't care. The urge to paint had gone away, thank God, leaving her emotionally drained. And so tired she thought she might keel over.

She had used pure crimson for the matador's cape. A few spots stained her white blouse and looked like blood. She hurt all over, as if she had been gored by the bull's horns. Still half-dazed, she dragged her aching body up the stairs, entered Gabe's bedroom, shed her clothes, and curled up under the blanket.

Behind her closed eyelids, she pictured matadors and picadors and banderillos. She wanted to cover her ears against the sound of clapping hands and stamping feet. She felt the tense, horrid expectation of the crowd and smelled the dust of the bullring—even though she'd never been to a bullfight, never even *watched* a bullfight.

Bullfights were brutal, bloody, and she knew—without a single doubt—that she'd feel a deep, emotional empathy for the bull.

Ivan had once told her to grow up, that bullfights were merely sporting events and that the bull had a better than even chance.

She didn't believe him, not for one moment.

If a movie began to depict a bullfight, she left the theatre. If the movie was on TV, she shut her eyes. Or turned off the TV.

Tossing and turning, Hallie tried to sleep. But even with her eyes shut, she couldn't turn off her painting.

Chapter Eleven

Gabe downshifted the Blazer.

"Teddy Roosevelt once described Cripple Creek as scenery that bankrupts the English language," he said. "But you've lacked language, English or otherwise, for more than a dozen bumpy miles. Have you lost your voice?"

"Yes," Hallie replied with a dreamy smile. At the same time, she admired the play of Gabe's thigh muscles as his laced hiking boots hit the clutch and brake pedals. White denim hugged his lean hips. His blue shirt was rolled up above his elbows, revealing muscular forearms. He had suggested she dress comfortably and casually, so an old faded pair of jeans hugged *her* hips.

Maybe she should have worn something spiffier. She had packed her favorite ankle-length smock dress, but unless she stuffed her feet into high-heeled boots, the smock was too long.

Allowing a dress to trail on the street is in exceedingly bad taste. Such a street costume simply calls forth criticism and contempt from more sensible people.

Despair coursed through her as she stifled the urge to plug her ears with her fingers. The voice was inside her head. Plugging her ears wouldn't help.

"I guess you can't talk and assimilate bumps at the same time," Gabe teased.

"New York has bumps, only we call them potholes," she

retorted. "Frankly, I'm trying to assimilate all this beauty. And the altitude. Both are making me lose my breath."

"You'll get used to the altitude."

"New York has mountains, the Catskills. Did you ever hear the joke about Rip van Winkle? When he awoke from his hundred-year nap, he found a phone and dialed his brokerage firm. The stockbroker who answered said, 'Mr. Winkle, your assets are now worth five billion dollars.' Rip was delighted. As a billionaire he could do all the things he'd never done before. Visit Europe. Wed a beautiful woman. Eat fine food and drink expensive wines. Then an operator interrupted his conversation. The operator said, 'Please deposit *one million dollars* for the first three minutes.' "

The sound of Gabe's laughter eradicated Hallie's despair. "I'm still sleepy," she admitted ruefully, yawning behind her hand. "And yet, I feel as if I slept a hundred years last night."

A bald-faced lie, she thought. Gabe's gaze was riveted on the road, so he couldn't see her eyes, heavy-lidded with fatigue and bright with denial. He hadn't discovered her bullfight painting because she'd risen early and primed the canvas with thick white primer, erasing the bull, the matador, the crowd and the little girl.

Despite her puzzling compulsion to create the original Cripple Creek scenes, the six resultant paintings had intrigued her. The bullfight painting, however, terrified her. She understood why the little girl screamed because she would have screamed, too, and that was the scary part. Somehow, she had stepped into her own painting and become the little girl.

Hallie shook her curls. No. She hadn't become the little girl. She'd felt a *connection* with the little girl.

Now she wished she had left the canvas unprimed. Gabe

had soothed her fears last night, so he might have a perfectly logical explanation for her latest paranormal pictorialization.

"I'm still sleepy," she repeated.

"It's the altitude, honey."

"You blame everything on the altitude, don't you?"

"Yup."

They reached the top of a steep rise. Hallie gazed down at what looked like haphazardly clustered houses and hotels, spread out across a Monopoly board. "Where did the name Cripple Creek come from?" she asked.

"A cow wandered across the creek, fell, and broke her leg."

"Really? That's the truth?"

"Cross my heart."

"Even from a distance the town looks so charming, so aesthetic. How can they allow gambling?"

"The favorite justification is that gambling played an integral part in Cripple Creek's history. It was the recreational release that gave men the resolve to go down into those mines day after day, month after month." Removing his hand from the steering wheel, Gabe gestured toward the Mollie Kathleen gold mine, now a tourist attraction.

Although she'd never been particularly claustrophobic, Hallie shuddered at the thought of entering its dark, dank concavity. Not her cup of tea.

"Some say you can hear the miners," Gabe continued, "coal-black from working underground all day, whooping it up at the poker tables. Cripple Creek is filled with ghosts."

So am I, thought Hallie, tightening the laces on her sneakers.

Gabe parked in a small lot behind a casino called Elk Creek, then retrieved his camera bag from the Blazer's backseat. "If you don't mind," he said, "I'd like to spend a few minutes with Elk Creek's owner, Joe. I've promised to shoot some photos for his decor."

"Boudoir photos?"

"Nope. Elk. Come to think of it, Joe might prefer one of your paintings."

"I don't paint elks."

Gabe laughed. "Elk, Hallie, singular. One elk, two elk, three elk."

"Okay, I don't paint *elk*."

"No, but you paint authentic scenes from turn-of-the-century Cripple Creek."

"I wouldn't take a job away from you, Gabe."

"Don't worry. Elk aren't my cup of tea."

"Holy Moses! I had that very same thought when I saw the Mollie Kathleen. Dark mines aren't my cup of tea. I don't even like to drive through New York's Holland Tunnel." She shuddered again.

"Speaking of tea," Gabe said, "are you thirsty?"

"I'm fine, thank you," she replied. "Let's go meet your friend."

Actually, she wasn't fine. She had honestly expected that her first sight of Cripple Creek would conjure up bygone images. Lady Scarlet. The little girl. Gabriel. She had anticipated joy, fearful anxiety, even the sorrowful ache she'd experienced when her mom had mentioned Myers Avenue. But she didn't feel anything except a vague curiosity, just like any ordinary out-of-towner.

That changed, however, when she followed Gabe through the open doors of the casino. Almost immediately, she was buffeted by strong winds, as if she'd entered a wind tunnel. A breathy voice chanted, "Come out, come out, wherever you are. Why are you hiding? Let's play hopscotch. Even better, let's bedevil the doorman at the Palace till he shoos us away."

Then the wind stopped and everything appeared normal, if a picturesque building filled with slot machines and blackjack tables could be considered normal.

"Where's the Palace?" Hallie asked, still somewhat dazed.

"At the end of the street," Gabe replied. "Why?"

"She's hungry, you dumb ox," said a bearded man with twinkly eyes. "The Palace Hotel has good food at reasonable prices. Right, Hallie?"

"I've never been there." She chewed her bottom lip, aware that Gabe must have introduced her to his friend while she'd been inside the wind tunnel. What had Gabe said before? His friend's name was . . . Jack? No. Something with a J. Oh, yes . . . Joe.

Ignoring the quizzical stares from both men, she blurted, "Gabe says Cripple Creek is filled with ghosts. Do you have any Elk Creek ghosts, Joe?"

"Yep. A little girl. She was trapped by the 1896 fire, and now her uncle wants her to stay inside the building while he searches for the rest of the family."

"No," Hallie corrected. "*She's* searching for her lost playmates. Your little girl ghost didn't die in the fire. I think she died much older, but haunts your casino as a child. Maybe she even haunts other saloons."

"Hallie has acute perceptions," said Gabe. "She's from New York," he added, as if that explained it. "In fact, she's done several Cripple Creek paintings for a New York gallery show. Hand over your snapshots, honey."

Joe studied the Polaroid photos, then whistled. "Forget the elk, Quinn. These are great. Have your gallery get in touch with me, Hallie. How about some hot dogs? On the house."

"Thanks," said Gabe, "but we plan to picnic by the side of the road. Before we eat, I'll let Hallie explore Cripple Creek. It's her first visit. She's never seen our ghostly town before."

Joe's brow furrowed. "If she's never seen Cripple Creek, how did she do her paintings? From old photos?"

"No, from memory," Gabe called over his shoulder, belting Hallie's waist with his fingers and escorting her outside.

"That was mean," she said, breathing in the brisk, sunshiny air. "Joe will think I'm some sort of psychic nut."

Gabe shook his head. "Joe will spread the word, and soon others will be bidding for your paintings."

"Why?"

"People love to collect the unexplainable. Ghosts, for instance."

"I'm not a ghost."

"Thank God. I don't hanker to kiss a ghost, ma'am." Tilting her chin with his first finger, Gabe pressed his lips against hers.

Hallie stumbled backwards. They were out in the open, surrounded by tourists. In fact, one carrot-haired little girl who looked like Pippi Longstocking was rudely pointing.

I'm overreacting, Hallie thought. *Marianne would say that Elmo introduced the K-word on "Sesame Street." K-for-kiss. K-for-kanoodle. No, you featherbrained mooncalf! C-for-canoodle.*

Canoodle?

Obsolete speak again!

Just the same, she *was* overreacting. On tiptoe, she gave Gabe a hearty smooch. He responded by gently pressing her face between his palms and deepening the kiss. His tongue began a sensuous tango with her tongue, and the sidewalk people vanished as she sought to prolong the embrace. Then the loud clink of coins brought her to her senses. Somebody inside Elk Creek had won a jackpot. The clinky sound continued while she blurted the first thing that came to mind. "Do you believe in ghosts, Gabe?"

"When I was a kid I believed in Casper, and I love watching Past, Present and Future perform their Scrooge magic every Christmas." Releasing her face, he circled her shoulders with his arm. "Would you like to stroll through the Old Homestead? It's the only parlor house that still exists."

"Yes, please. Where is it?"

"Myers Avenue."

"We're not on Myers?"

"We're on Bennett. Myers runs parallel."

They walked a block, and this time Hallie did feel the fearful anxiety she had anticipated. She also lost her breath, at least temporarily. She opened her mouth to tell Gabe, but bit back her words. Why ruin what was turning out to be a wonderful day? Her dream man's hand rested on the sleeve of her red and blue striped turtleneck and her breasts pushed against the shirt's cotton as if they had a life of their own, as if they hoped for an accidental caress. Furthermore, Gabe had just sold at least one of her canvases and her gallery show hadn't even opened yet.

If honest, she had to admit she'd become infatuated with Gabriel, the man in her painting. But now she preferred the man who walked by her side, guiding her toward the parlor house. A painting couldn't evoke Gabe Quinn's intelligence. Or his compassion. Or his sense of humor. A painting couldn't circle her shoulders and send shivery sensations up and down her spine. A painting couldn't make her breasts throb and her legs melt. A painting couldn't cause the chaste maiden to forget all about guarding Vesta's fire and concentrate, instead, on the fire inside her own belly, a fire that extended to the very core of her sensations. "Tell it like it is," Marianne would say. "You want this guy."

"Here she sets," Gabe announced, "in all her quiet dignity. The Old Homestead."

"It's much smaller than *my* parlor house. The one I painted. The Homestretch."

"But much more famous. Or should I say infamous? The Old Homestead enjoyed the finest trade, gave the grandest soirees, and achieved the greatest sophistication of any brothel in the gold camp. The Homestead's girls were the scorched toast of the town."

"My parlor girls aren't scorched."

"How can you say that? They slept with the miners."

"No, Gabe, they entertained the miners."

"What's the difference?"

"Survival versus sin. Let's go inside."

"After you."

Hallie entered and glanced around. "Holy Moses! Look at all those objets d'art. I'd love to buy some for my apartment. *Sacre bleu,* talk about unique!"

"Unfortunately, my pretty *French* toast, they're not for sale."

Together, Gabe and Hallie strolled upstairs. Five bedrooms were on display, furnished with patchwork quilts, brass beds, and marble-topped dressers. Several mannequins stood guard. They all wore authentic clothes from the late nineteenth century.

Wandering into one of the bedrooms, Hallie's gaze touched upon a dressing table, cluttered with bottles and trinkets. She felt a finger tap her shoulder. The finger was very cold, very stiff. Startled, she whirled about.

A pasty-faced mannequin with sparse blonde hair said, "Don't steal anything, you brat."

Another mannequin said, "Leave her alone."

The first mannequin said, "The last time you visited, my bottle of hair restorer left with you."

"Knickers would never take your damnfool bottle," the

second mannequin retorted. "Her curls are so thick I can't hardly comb out the tangles."

"Scarlet," the pasty-faced mannequin said, "the child's a thief."

"The child's an angel!" the mannequin named Scarlet exclaimed.

"Her papa stole," said Pasty-Face.

"He stole my heart."

"And your money," Pasty-Face said. "Every cent."

"He didn't steal my money. He borrowed it."

The first mannequin laughed. "He walked away seven years ago and never came home. I don't call that borrowing."

"My papa died digging for gold, you hatchet-faced harlot," Hallie cried. "A bear et him." She fisted her hands. "Take it back or you'll be puking up teeth!"

"Honey?" Staring down at the tense figure standing by his side, Gabe saw that her eyes were out of focus and her hands were clenched into fists. Frightened, he grasped her elbow and steered her down the stairs, then outside, into the brilliant sunlight. "Hallie, wake up!"

"A bear et him," she repeated. "If you shoot the dang bear and cut open his stomach, you'll find my papa—"

"Hallie O'Brien!"

"—just like Jonah and Red Riding Hood."

Gabe felt totally at a loss. How could he reach her? People had slowed or stopped, gawking at the angry woman who sounded like a child.

Hallie turned toward them. "Staring at somebody, spitting, looking back after they pass, calling out loudly, or laughing at somebody as they go by, are all evidence of ill-breeding."

Facing Gabe, she said, "A gentleman walking with a lady

should accommodate his step and pace to hers. For the gent to be some distance ahead presents a bad appearance."

Gabe decided to play along. "That's right, Hallie."

"Knickers. My name, as you very well know, is Knickers."

"Sorry, little one. I'll accommodate my step and pace to yours while we walk to my car. Okay?"

"Carriage, silly. Trains have cars." She yawned, blushed, covered her mouth with her hand, yawned again. Then she swept imaginary hair over one shoulder. "Okay," she said. "We'll walk to your carriage, Gabriel. Gentlemen must take their seat with their backs to the horses, care being observed that gowns and shawls are not shut in the door when it's closed. Last week you shut my petticoat in the door," she chided.

Leading Hallie away from the Old Homestead, Gabe heard a woman say, "I'll bet that was a performance. Ain't she cute?"

Cute? he mused. *Not hardly.* "We've almost reached the car . . . carriage," he said, "but you look exhausted. Do you want to ride piggyback?"

"What did you say?"

Stopping short, Gabe glanced down. Hallie's eyes were alert, focused. "You've been yawning," he said, "so I thought you might like to ride—"

"Piggyback? When did we leave the parlor house? I tranced again, didn't I? Oh, God! Why is this happening to me?"

"To us," he said.

"No, Gabe, me. You don't lose your sensibilities."

"Yes, I do," he teased, "every time we kiss. But I promise we'll solve this puzzle, Hallie. For starters, we now know the little girl's name."

Chapter Twelve

"Her name is Knickers? Are you sure?"

"That's enough, Hallie. We'll discuss this after we eat."

"But you wouldn't let me talk about it in the car, and—"

"Later."

Fuming, she watched Gabe spread an orange and blue blanket across the grassy ground. Then he hunkered down and yanked open a cooler.

"Look, honey," he said, "live lobsters. Big ones."

"You're kidding, right?"

"Yup. I packed turkey sandwiches, cheese, fruit, soda and beer."

"A beer sounds great."

"I don't think so."

"Why not?"

"The altitude. A beer would go straight to your head."

"Really! How can *you* drink it?"

"Altitude doesn't affect me. I'm a native Coloradan."

"So am I."

"What happened to New Yorker, born and bred?"

Momentarily, she fell silent. Then she said, "I was joking, paying you back for the lobster."

No, you weren't, Gabe thought, but decided to let it pass. He wanted her to eat and relax, especially relax. Her whole body was drawn tighter than an arrow through a bowstring.

He'd chosen their picnic site with care. High above Cripple Creek, the secluded glen was surrounded by dense brush and a profusion of wildflowers that scented the atmosphere with a musty cologne, as if Nature had created a department store cosmetics counter and sprayed the air with sample perfume. Should people below happen to glance up, they'd merely see aspen trees, shimmering with orange-gold splendor.

Sitting on her heels, Hallie nibbled at a wedge of cheese. Then she avidly consumed the cheese, a sandwich, and three purple grapes.

"I was hungry," she understated with a smile. "Hungry as a bear."

The perfect opening. Should he mention the bear-et-Papa bit?

"How do you feel now?" he asked, instead.

"Sleepy."

"Stay awake!"

"Not trance sleepy, Gabe. Ordinary sleepy. Can we talk about what happened at the Old Homestead?"

"Where do your parents come from?"

"What does that have to do with . . . oh. This might be a generational thing?"

"Maybe," he replied.

"My dad was born in Brooklyn. His folks emigrated from Ireland. My mom's a second-generation New Yorker."

"And your great-grandparents? On your mother's side?"

"My great-grandfather came from Texas. I'm not sure about Granny Bea. She was something else, my great-grandmother. Just like your father, she fought for civil rights, only she waged her battle long before organized protests were established. Her name was Beatrice, but they called her Bea. She had a brief fling as a singer, even performed a solo in one of Ziegfeld's shows. Then she challenged the theatre's segregation policy and that was the end of her showbiz career."

"You said you couldn't sing. Right?"

Hallie nodded, her curls bobbing. "My mom can carry a tune, but I can't carry a note. My dad has a marvelous voice, very vibratory, an Irish Elvis. Aren't we contemplating my mother's side of the family?"

"Yes. The 1890s. Did your great-grandmother have sisters? Brothers?"

"I don't know. Granny Bea was adopted." Hallie moved closer to Gabe, who was sitting with his back propped against the trunk of a tree. "I don't feel sad or anxious, and yet I have a feeling I've been here before."

"With me or Gabriel?"

"Gabriel. Does that make you angry?"

"No, not really. But I would prefer a flesh and blood rival."

"You have no rival, Gabe, cross my heart."

"Good idea," he said, drawing her body into his lap. "I think your heart's over here, maybe higher. Where do you put your hand when you salute the flag?"

"Where do you put yours?" she countered.

He tugged her shirt free from the waistband of her jeans, unsnapped her bra, then pressed his hand against her left breast. "I pledge allegiance to your heart," he murmured, circling her swollen nipple with his thumb.

"I'm losing my breath again," she gasped, "and don't blame it on the altitude. Please kiss me, Gabe."

"That won't restore your breath."

"I don't care. Who needs breath?"

"Not me. Let's lose our breath together."

The tree trunk provided support as Gabe propped Hallie against his drawn-up knees, cradled her chin with both hands, then slowly, deliberately, traced her mouth with the tip of his tongue until he felt the soft, moist, inner edges of her lips yield.

* * * * *

r nails into Gabe's shoulders, Hallie felt his fin- n gently thrust through her open fly. Panting, she and forth, silently urging his fingers to increase their pressure. A whimper escaped through her parted lips.

Would Gabe never unzip *his* jeans and ease her throbbing ache with something harder, stronger, thicker than a finger? Her body began to quiver with bursts of uncontrollable pleasure. Totally unnerved, she loosened her hold on Gabe's shoulders and let her heavy head fall backwards.

Time stood still. Nothing moved. She saw the treetops. Not one branch stirred, not one leaf rustled. She saw birds suspended in the sky. Not one wing flapped in flight. She felt Gabe withdraw his fingers.

Leaves rustled. Birds circled the clouds.

"What's wrong?" She dug her nails into his shoulders again.

"Beast."

Confused, she stared into his eyes. "As in soothe the savage?" Then she remembered. "Oh, your brother."

"Beast loves you, Hallie."

Staggering to her feet, she fumbled at her bra hooks and rezipped her jeans. "Josh has built up this fairy tale image of Sleeping Hallie, and he wants to fight dragons or scale castle walls until he can kiss her awake. But you're the only one who can kiss me awake, Gabe. Don't you love me a little?" she asked plaintively.

"I think I love you a lot."

"Enough to fight dragons?"

"Yes."

"Enough to fight a flesh and blood rival?"

"I won't fight my brother." Rising, he began to collect the picnic items. "But I will reason with him, explain how I feel."

"How *we* feel. This is happening to us, remember?"

"Speaking of remember, do you remember anything from your dream states?"

"Trances, Gabe. Please don't be subtle."

"Do you remember anything, Hallie?"

"No. Except for the wind tunnel inside Elk Creek, which wasn't really a trance, and the one in New York, when my sister-in-law gave birth. I delivered her baby. Why are you grinning? Don't you think I can deliver a baby?"

"Of course I do."

"If you say it's because I'm a woman or because I have maternal instincts, I'll strangle you. That's what Ivan . . . what a friend of my brother's said. 'Since women *have* the babies, they know how to deliver them,' he said. I only wish *he* could carry a baby around for nine months. And go into labor!"

"Tell me what happened when your sister-in-law gave birth."

"I called her Scarlet and mentioned Gabriel and I think I saw Knickers. She was about to boil some water." Hallie sighed. "My paintings are the clues, Gabe, but I don't feel the compulsion to paint right now. I feel peaceful, happy. Maybe that's because I've been here before. There was a cabin, not far from this very spot. I can see a crude corral, a shed for the horses, an outhouse, a vegetable garden, and a clothesline."

"A clothesline," he echoed.

"Yes. I see drawers hanging from—"

"Drawers?"

"Not bureau or desk drawers. Panties. Loose-fitting panties gathered at the knees. That's how our little girl got her nickname." Hallie stared into the distance. "Knickers lived in the cabin, along with her pets. And Gabriel."

"No, honey. Knickers lived in a parlor house. Dammit, listen to me. I'm talking as if she really existed."

"She did exist." Hallie auditioned a smile. "But I think she might have grown some before she shared the cabin with Gabriel. I think they were lovers."

"And I think you're letting your imagination run wild."

"Well, there's one way to find out. We'll simply bide our time until my next painting. What are your plans for tonight?"

He glanced down at his watch. "It's three-thirty. I want to shoot a roll of film before the sun sets, then drive to Woodland Park. I promised Josh we'd pick up a pizza and rent some videos. He promised he'd secure Napkin in the yard."

"That's not necessary. I like dogs."

"Do you like slobber? Pizza just happens to be Napkin's favorite snack. He'll even eat the box. That reminds me. Josh mentioned a hypnotherapist—"

"No! No way, Gabe! I don't want to go into a trance. I want to come out of one."

"More than one. What are you afraid of?"

"I'm not afraid. Sunsets scare me, not some stupid spellbinder."

"Sunsets scare you?"

"Did I say sunsets? I meant . . ." She paused, very close to tears. "I don't know what I meant."

"Hush," he soothed. "I'll protect you from sunsets. And dragons. Okay?"

Nodding, she watched him bend and retrieve the blanket. Then she grasped one end and walked backwards. Folding the blanket lengthwise, she stepped toward him, until their eyes met and their fingers touched.

"You're right, Gabe. I'm afraid of a hypnotist." Dropping the blanket, she squeezed his hands. "I'm afraid I might never wake up."

He released his end of the blanket, disentangled her fingers from his hands, pressed her face against his shoulder, and gently massaged her shoulders.

I'm afraid I might not want to, she thought.

Chapter Thirteen

It's Monopoly time again, Hallie mused. *Colorado Monopoly. You can land on Bennett or Myers Avenue, rather than Park Place or Boardwalk.. Pass Go, collect $200, throw the dice, and advance to Woodland Park, a picturesque municipality where the mountains rise up above God's feet and tickle his knees.*

Joshua Quinn's house looked like a Monopoly house. Small and red, it boasted gingerbread trim painted lavender, salmon and teal. The trim proclaimed that an artist lived there, perhaps even the very same artist who had created the illustrations for a popular *Hansel and Gretel* book, where the children were black and the witch was white and the colorful candy-coated cottage stood within a maze of tenements. A much more effective message than "Just say no."

Stepping from the Blazer, Hallie stretched while Gabe retrieved a large pizza box and four video tapes, leaving his camera bag on the backseat. The bag's zippered compartment held rolls of film, ready for processing. Gabe had clicked away while she assumed various poses. But she wasn't a professional model. Despite his encouragement, she'd felt unnatural, stiff, as if she were an Old Homestead mannequin.

How could he use those photos in his catalogue, especially since she'd worn her turtleneck and jeans? He had emphatically stated that she didn't need to slip on the authentic nineteenth-century clothes he'd brought along.

Was he afraid she might retreat into one of her trances?

When developed, would Gabe's pictures elicit the same emotions she had experienced at the glen? The feeling that she'd been there before? Happy? Cherished? Loved?

After driving away from Cripple Creek, those feelings had diminished. Well, not really. Because Gabe evoked the very same sensations, not to mention lustful exultation.

Lustful exultation? Holy Moses! "Tell it like it is, kiddo," Marianne would say. " 'Sesame Street' 's Elmo introduced the O-word yesterday."

During her few brief moments of unrestricted passion, Hallie had experienced pulsating bursts of pleasure. But now she wanted more. She wanted fulfillment. If fulfilled, would she explode? *People don't explode except verbally.* Wrong! She'd been on the verge until Gabriel suddenly developed scruples.

Gabe, not Gabriel. Why couldn't she keep them straight?

Bringing her attention back to *Gabe,* she saw that he was striding up the cobblestone path. "Hey, Beast," he yelled, "hide your dog!"

Too late. A cross between a Shetland pony and a grizzly bear threw his weight against the screen door. It opened, and Napkin leaped the porch steps in a single bound. Faster than a speeding bullet, he hurled himself toward them—a furry, canine Michael Jordan.

Hallie scurried up the path and rescued the video tapes while Gabe shielded his chest with the pizza box.

Undaunted, the pony-bear reared up and washed Gabe's face with a tongue the size of a small skateboard.

Josh stumbled onto the porch. Abruptly summoned by Gabe's and Hallie's arrival, he had vacated his shower. Dripping wet, he wore a pair of Taz boxer shorts. "Napkin," he shouted, "get in the house!"

"Napkin, get down!" Gabe ordered sternly.

"Napkin, get inside!"

"Beast, get dressed!"

"What? Oh." Josh disappeared.

Overcome with the giggles, Hallie watched Gabe and Napkin perform a dance that was half-jitterbug, half-waltz.

The pizza box had been flung skyward and it now decorated the lawn. Incredibly, it was still intact. Should she rescue the pizza? Or Gabe?

Before she could make a decision, Josh appeared again. He had thrown on jeans and a plaid shirt, unbuttoned. In his hand he clutched three large dog biscuits. "C'mon, baby," he pleaded. "Look, baby, biscuits. C'mon, baby."

Baby? Hallie couldn't help it. Doubled over with laughter, she sank to the ground. A big mistake. Napkin abandoned Gabe and loomed above her. Beethoven with an attitude. The movie dog, not the composer.

"Biscuits!" Josh yelled, his voice desperate.

"Pizza!" Gabe shouted, snatching up the box.

"Napkin, get in the house," Hallie said, her voice firm.

The dog stopped growling, turned tail, and walked meekly up the porch steps. Then he sat, waiting for someone to open the door.

"How'd you do that?" Gabe extended his hand and helped her rise.

"New York has animals bigger than Napkin, only we call them wolves. Human wolves. The best way to deal with a wolf is to never beg and never show fear." Despite her brave words, she began to tremble.

"Right." Dropping the pizza box next to the scattered video tapes, Gabe drew her into his arms. "Beast," he said, "get rid of that stupid mutt."

"I once enrolled Napkin in an obedience class," Josh muttered. "They used dog biscuits as a reward. Napkin toppled the trainer and chomped down every biscuit. Then he threw up all over a Chihuahua named Peewee. Peewee's owner threatened to sue."

The bang of the screen door emphasized Josh's last words.

Gabe pressed Hallie's face against his shoulder. "Delayed reaction, honey?"

"No. More like emotional stress. I couldn't stop laughing and now I'm crying. If there was a Chihuahua handy, I'd probably throw up."

"Poor baby."

"Baby?" She started laughing again. "Josh called Napkin baby," she gasped between giggles. "Did you hear him?"

Alarmed, Gabe held Hallie at arm's length. Her eyes still brimmed with tears, but her laughter continued bubbling up and spilling over. If she didn't stop soon, she really would become sick. Should he slap her face? No. He couldn't. He'd never slapped a woman's face. Frustrated, he followed his only other impulse. Cradling her cheeks with his palms, he lowered his head and kissed her mouth.

Her laughter subsided as she molded her lips to his. At the same time, she reached up to wind her arms around his neck. Gabe felt her lips part. Thrusting his tongue inside, he savored her sweet breath. Although sheathed by a shirt and bra, he could feel her nipples harden. Releasing his mouth, she licked the scar that adorned his chin.

The sun was sinking fast, but they were out in the open. He hesitated. Then passion replaced reason. Sensation consumed sanity. Belting Hallie's waist with his hands, he lifted her off the ground and carried her toward porch shadows.

Sobbing anew, this time with desire, she straddled his hips.

His fingers traveled down her spine. When they reached

her buttocks, he maneuvered one hand between her spread thighs and pressed, as hard as he could, against her zippered fly.

She whimpered and Napkin barked. Her breathy whimper came from deep down inside her throat. Napkin's strident bark came from the backyard. Which meant, thought Gabe, that his brother would reappear any minute.

"Josh," he whispered into her ear.

Hallie shivered. Gabe's breath had created new ripples of desire. But she merely unstraddled his waist. As her sneakers touched the path, she tried to regain her composure.

"I wish . . ." she began.

Gabe said, "You wish what?"

"I wish we were Knickers and Gabriel, snuggled together inside their cabin."

"We'll snuggle later."

She shook her head. "Josh would know if we . . . snuggled. It would show." Striving for humor, she said, "I've never felt this way before, so impulsive, so uninhibited. Do you think it's the altitude?"

Chapter Fourteen

Hallie stared skeptically at the pizza box that decorated Josh's glass coffee table. Cheese stuck to the top of the box and cold grease saturated its bottom. Earth-stained paw prints almost obliterated the cardboard's red logo.

"Have you warned her about the altitude?" Josh asked Gabe

"Yup," he said. "But I think Hallie and I both need a drink. Your damn mutt played tic-tac-toe on my chest with his nails. And he scared Hallie breathless."

Great ad-lib, she thought, still breathless from Gabe's kiss.

"I've got a bottle of chilled champagne," Josh said, his expression smug.

Gabe quirked an eyebrow. "What's the occasion? Your new contract?"

"Nope. Join me in the kitchen, Scarecrow. Please excuse us, Hallie. You can choose the first movie. Okay?"

"Okay." She walked over to the video machine, on top of the TV.

Gabe followed his brother through an arched doorway. "Why the champagne? What's up, Beast?"

"I'm so embarrassed, Scarecrow. I've made such a fuss over Hallie O'Brien, bent your ear countless times, but what I felt was infatuation."

"Infatuation," Gabe repeated, dumbfounded.

"That's right. When true love strikes, it takes your breath away."

"Breath away."

"And who do you think causes me to lose my breath? None other than Kayla Partridge."

"Kayla Partridge."

"Must you repeat everything I say?"

"Who's Kayla Partridge?"

"My princess. The girl next door. When Kayla posed for Puss in Boots, she was in high school. Now she's in college."

"Aha!" Gabe grinned. "Do you love her?"

"I think so. At least I've got all the symptoms."

"Does she love you?"

"Not yet. But she will. I'll woo her with candy, flowers and books."

"Poetry?"

"No. My books."

"Children's books?"

"Yup. How can she resist?"

"You love the girl next door." Gabe laughed. "That's wonderful."

"Will you do me yet another huge favor, Scarecrow?"

"Anything. Name it."

"I told Hallie I would show her the sights, but Kayla's only planning to be here a few days. Then she goes back to school. I hate to ask, but would you look after Hallie?"

"Absolutely. Gladly. Not a problem." Laughing again, Gabe ruffled his brother's hair. "Silly old Beast."

From the living room, Hallie heard the sound of Gabe's laughter. He had a nice laugh. He had a nice everything. With a sigh, she studied the rental tapes. She'd been surprised when Gabe suggested *The Princess Bride.* Hallie adored the William Goldman–scripted movie and found new things to grin over every time she watched it.

The other tapes were action-adventure flicks, starring Keanu Reeves, Samuel Jackson, and Charles Bronson. Marianne loved old Bronson movies, but Hallie hated them. If Bronson established any kind of relationship, his girlfriend almost always got killed. Were a few weeks, months, even years of rapture worth getting killed for? Or was it better to die of old age, a rapture-less spinster?

"My brother likes movies with car chases and explosions," Gabe had said inside the video store. "But I've seen enough death and destruction."

Death and destruction! The words sounded familiar. Of course they did. Hadn't her mom used those very same words to describe Cripple Creek's saloons and brothels?

"Where did you see death and destruction, Gabe?" she had asked.

"I was once a photojournalist."

"Photojourn . . . ohmigosh! They . . . everyone called you Gabriel Q. I've seen your war photos." Excitement building, she said, "I've even seen you in *Newsweek*. You looked different. Your hair was shorter. You had a mustache and beard. That's why I didn't recognize you. At the airport. But I read the *Newsweek* article, so my portrait was probably—"

"Subliminal? No. I don't believe that anymore. You didn't paint me. You painted Gabriel."

Hallie brought her attention back to the tapes at hand. Should she honor her host and choose an action movie? Before she could decide, Gabe and Josh reentered the room. Both were grinning from ear to ear.

"Forget the videos," Gabe said, "and join us in a toast."

Puzzled, Hallie accepted a goblet filled with champagne.

"To love," said Gabe.

"To love," said Josh.

"To love," Hallie echoed.

But other words reverberated inside her head. Words that made her heart rise and beat against the pulse at the base of her throat. Words that, had she said them out loud, would have strangled her.

Death and destruction, death and destruction, death and . . .

Chapter Fifteen

"I warned you about the altitude," Gabe said. Circling Hallie's waist, he guided her toward the front door.

"Bilgewater," she stated indignantly.

"Bilgewater?"

"Horsefeathers, Gabe. The altitude's not affectin' me. You are." A bemused smile spread across her face. "I had to toast love, didn't I? Then I toasted Josh and his princess. Then the princess bride and Keanu and make-my-day Charlie."

"Make my day was Clint. Do you remember anything about the Keanu Reeves movie?" Gabe's voice was filled with amusement.

"Not much," she admitted. "I wanted to leave so badly. I'm going to pose for you, and this time I'll model like a model. Not a mannequin."

Ushering Hallie inside, Gabe kicked the door shut. "What are you talking about?"

"Boudoir photos. You have clothes from the nineteenth century. I saw camisoles and negligees when I painted my bullfight."

"You painted a bullfight?"

"I primed the canvas with white primer, so it's all gone. The bull won't die and the little girl can stop screaming."

"When did you paint a bullfight?"

"Last night. You were sleeping. You looked so handsome, so sculpted, like an ad for an exercise machine. But I wouldn't charge for handling, Gabe, not one red cent."

"Hallie, you're tipsy," he said, bathing the hallway with subdued illumination.

"I feel fine, Mr. Q. Please shoot me."

"I'll shoot a few *pictures* of you. After that, it's off to bed. Okay? Promise?"

"Cross my heart." She pressed his hand against her left breast, smiled again, then turned and raced toward the costume alcove.

Fumbling for the light switch, she felt her heart beat wildly, and the loud thump wasn't effectuated by champagne, or even the brief press of Gabe's warm hand. Up until tonight, events had been so serious. Now it was time to have some fun.

In other words, the chaste maiden wanted to be chased. And caught.

Momentarily, she wondered if she was really and truly the pragmatic Alice W. O'Brien her family knew and loved. Maybe she had shed her skin. Like a snake.

No. She'd shed her mind, her brain. In the romance novels she borrowed from Marianne, the hero and heroine didn't make love until chapter fifteen or sixteen, well into the book. First they messed around a little, until they were interrupted by a gunshot. Or the heroine's maiden aunt. Or the hero's horse . . .

Or the hero's scruples.

Gabe had scruples. She didn't know all that much about him, but she knew that much.

So *she* would have to initiate the seduction.

She pictured Neil's shocked expression. "It isn't as if Gabe and I just met," she told her brother's image. "We met a hundred years ago. A hundred years is a long pause, wouldn't you agree? And I don't care if that's a justification, Neil. It's a legitimate justification. And, to be perfectly honest, I don't want to wait until chapter sixteen."

What should she wear? The white camisole? No. Much too demure. How about the delicate pink peignoir? It was sheer, but it cloaked her legs. Legs. Stockings. Black net stockings had been draped over a clothes rack. Inside a bureau drawer, she found garters and several white velvet ribbons. Yes. Definitely ribbons. Shedding her jeans, she drew the stockings up her legs and tied the ribbons in bows, well above her knees. That kept the stockings in place, but now her white cotton undies looked ridiculous. A pair of red silk panties complemented the lacy white camisole, which, in retrospect, was not the least bit demure.

Did she look like a woman of easy virtue? Or a bratty kid playing dress-up? Gabe's expression would reveal the truth, the whole truth, and nothing but the truth.

Gabe's expression revealed nothing. He was busy adjusting lights and checking his camera for exposure settings.

"I'm ready," she purred.

"Hop up onto the platform, honey. There are props to your left. A teddy bear, a painted fan, a feathered boa. You choose."

She snatched up the teddy bear and struck what she hoped was a provocative pose.

Gabe was all business. "Relax," he said.

"I *am* relaxed."

"No, you're not. If I bent you over, you'd break in half, like a dry stick. Lean back a little and hold the bear against your cheek. Now you're hiding your face. Let's try some music."

"Maybe I need some more champagne," she shot back, cheeks aflame, the bear dangling from her fingertips.

"Champagne's the last thing you need. I want you alert, not droopy. Are you crying? What's wrong?"

"I look stu-stupid."

"You look stunning."

"I should have worn the peignoir."

"Aw, don't." Leaping up onto the platform, Gabe gathered her into his arms.

"I wanted to look sexy," she murmured against his shirt.

"Hallie, you'd look sexy if you wore a gunny sack."

"Really?"

"Cross my heart."

She heard the smile in his voice. "Prove it," she said, winding her arms, teddy bear and all, around his neck.

"I'll prove it with my photos."

"I think *you're* sexy, and I'm not a photographer."

"I'll shoot you tomorrow," he said. "I think it's time for bed."

"Put me to bed. No. Put me to couch. Don't you want me, Gabe?"

His reply was a long, slow exploration of her mouth that left her gasping for breath. Then he scooped her up and carried her to the couch.

"I want to touch you," she said, dropping the teddy bear. "I want to touch you all over."

Gabe placed her on the couch, shed his clothes, and lay next to her. "This couch isn't very big," he said, unbuttoning her camisole. "Wouldn't you be more comfortable upstairs?"

"There's plenty of room," she murmured, "if you climb on top."

"Oh, no, my love. We've got things to do before I climb."

"What things?"

Sliding from the couch, Gabe knelt. Very slowly, very deliberately, he untied her stocking bows, his fingers lingering. After drawing the stockings down her legs, over her ankles and feet, he stroked her inner thighs.

"What a waste of time, choosing an outfit," she murmured.

"That's part of the fun," he said.

"Choosing an outfit?"

"Taking it off."

"I didn't give you much to take off."

"You gave me enough."

He pulled her panties below her belly button, then circled the small indentation with his tongue. A throb began between her thighs, and she felt her nipples grow taut. "I want to touch you," she cried.

"Soon. I need to get you wet first."

"Why?"

"It will hurt less."

"I don't plan to hurt."

"You have no choice, little one. Unfortunately, it's not an option. I wish it were."

"Ohmigod! You know. How?"

"Last night you said you were pure."

"I did?"

"Yup. Don't look at me like that. I'm not turned off. I feel awed. And honored."

"Have you bedded virgins before?"

"One."

"The girl who called you a frog?"

"No. That was the fifth grade. I had the desire but not the technology."

Gently, he stroked her eyelids, forcing her to shut her eyes. Then he turned her head sideways and licked her inner ear. She tried to pull away from this new, intimate invasion, but his tongue probed deeper and deeper. Aroused beyond belief, she arched her back and thrust her breasts forward.

"Good girl," he whispered, his lips moving from her ear to her breasts.

She felt liquid fire slide throughout her body. Gabe licked

her nipples. Then he sucked her heart breast until she was nearly crazed with desire. Vaguely, she understood that he was waiting for her to indicate which portion of her body she wanted him to taste next. A difficult task since every portion of her body cried out for his attention. Furthermore, she wanted to taste him, or at least touch him. Soon, he'd said. But soon had no meaning when, without conscious thought, she brought her knees up and dug her heels into the couch.

"Good girl," he repeated, drawing her panties down until he reached her ankles, then waiting for her to thrust her feet toward the ceiling. Quickly, he tossed her panties aside and climbed onto the couch. When her feet descended, her legs were draped over his shoulders and his mouth was just below her navel. Frightened, she whimpered.

Rising to his feet, Gabe lowered her legs. "I'm sorry," he said. "I wanted to make you wet but I didn't mean to scare you."

He reached for the discarded teddy bear and placed the plush animal between her thighs, making sure its button eyes stared at the ceiling.

Up on the stage, the teddy bear had looked and felt lifeless, inanimate, impassive.

Hallie didn't feel lifeless or inanimate . . .

Nor did she feel impassive.

What was the opposite of impassive? Expressive?

Writhing pleasurably, she panted in short gasps, her tongue pressed against one corner of her lips.

Gabe moved the teddy bear's furry pelt back and forth, applying more and more pressure, until she was slick with her own moisture.

Consumed by exquisite sensations, at first she didn't realize that Gabe had removed the bear and straddled her hips. Then she felt new fur, Gabe's fur. In the midst of his fur, his erection rose hot and hard against her belly. With a moan, she thrust her breasts closer to the warmth of his lips and tongue.

Lifting his face, he said, "Tell me what you want."

"I want . . . to touch you," she panted.

"Where?"

"Here." She traced his buttocks. "And here." She wedged her fingers between their bodies until she had him firmly in the grasp of her hand. "Holy Moses! It's so big. Does it fit?"

Gabe swallowed his laughter. "Let's find out," he said as he began to penetrate.

"It doesn't fit," she said mournfully.

"Lord, Hallie, you're adorable." This time, he allowed his laughter to spill over. "Wind your legs around my waist, honey, and ride me like you'd ride a horse."

"I'm from New York," she said. "I've never ridden a horse in my life."

"How about a rocking horse?"

"Oh. Yes. I can do that."

She seesawed back and forth. As Gabe penetrated deeper, he heard her gasp with pain.

"I'll pull out," he said.

"No," she protested. "Give me a minute." She held her breath, released it slowly, then began to rock again.

Gabe adjusted his rhythm to hers. He felt her first flex, an instinctive tightening of muscles reluctant to give way. He felt her second contraction, a stretching. He felt her third contraction, and finally a series of violent quivers. Then her muscles were stroking him inside her as he thrust again and again, until their two bodies blended into one joyful hymn of deliverance.

"That was the first time for both of us," he murmured, his lips caressing the dimple that lurked below the sensual curve of her kiss-bruised mouth.

Chapter Sixteen

Hallie opened her eyes.

She lay on Gabe's bed, her body dovetailed against his. Gabe's hand palmed her left breast, his index finger resting near her nipple, as if he crossed her heart. She smiled. From now on the phrase "cross my heart" would have a significant meaning.

Tempted to wake her heart-crosser and practice anew the pleasurable sensations he inspired, she felt her fingers curl around an imaginary paintbrush.

Not now. Oh, please, not now. Rather than smearing canvas with her brush, she wanted to paint Gabe's rock-hard chest with her tongue. She wanted his tongue to erase bothersome Cripple Creek images and bring her to the very brink of forgetful ecstasy.

That was what he'd done the second time. Which, he said afterwards, was the first time all over again, minus her pain. No longer timid, she had urged his entry, rising up to meet his thrusts, memorizing the contours of his buttocks with her heels. Their frenzied motions caused the back-less, arm-less couch to topple over. Laughing, Gabe had carried her upstairs, into his bedroom. There, she'd soared toward the starry skylight while they finished her second lesson in love.

Now she felt like purring. Song lyrics couldn't begin to capture her emotions. She needed a whole orchestra: violins and thundering snare drums and the vibratory clash of cymbals. During her sojourn through galaxies called Desire, Passion and Ecstasy, she'd heard the orchestra. She had also heard a young girl whispering, "It was worth the wait, Gabriel," but she had ignored that whisper by letting Gabe's hands and lips consume all coherent thought.

With a sigh, she rose from the bed. Where was her bra? Downstairs. Forget the bra. Her compulsion to paint had become overwhelming.

Donning her raggedy T-shirt and denim shorts, she exited the bedroom and raced toward the costume alcove.

Usually Gabe slept like the proverbial log. But an almost unbearable sense of loss brought him fully awake. The overhead skylight showed a few stars: light, bright, wishing stars. Sitting up, he lifted his hand, planning to caress Hallie's perfumed curls.

She was gone.

Okay, he warned himself, don't panic. She wasn't gone for good. If she had "tranced," her body would still be lying next to him. Perhaps, thirsty, she'd wandered into the bathroom or kitchenette. And why was he just sitting here, like some damn bump on some damn log?

He never wore pajamas. Where was his robe? Downstairs, on top of the family room sofa, along with Monday night's blanket and pillow. He hadn't planned to share Hallie's bed, not even after his brother's confession. It was too soon, even if *she* thought they'd known each other for a hundred years. Her Gabriel memories didn't count. He wasn't Gabriel.

Then she had posed for his camera, posed for *him,* bathed in lights that had turned her velvety skin amber. She had pressed a teddy bear against her breasts. Lucky bear, he had thought, trying to remain stoic, impassive, until she said, "Don't you want me, Gabe?"

Yes, he wanted her. He wanted to kiss her nonstop and

erase the past. Permanently. He had a feeling her trances were very risky. What if she lapsed into one and couldn't come out of it?

Rising from the bed, he yanked open a bureau drawer and retrieved a pair of jeans that were air-conditioned at the knees. Stuffing his right leg into the jeans, hopping on his left leg, he suddenly realized that his left leg felt strong and whole, nary a trace of the stiffness he usually experienced after strenuous exercise.

Strenuous exercise? Hallie had done all the legwork. He hadn't exactly busted a gut while removing her camisole. He hadn't exactly strained an arm or wrist muscle while stripping off her stockings and panties. He hadn't exactly knocked himself out by nuzzling her supremely supple body.

On the other hand, he had downshifted the Blazer, walked through the streets of Cripple Creek, danced with Napkin, and carried Hallie upstairs.

Maybe the doctors were right. Maybe all those months of disciplined swimming and weight lifting had fortified his muscles. If he could leap and bound again, he need only make a few phone calls—

Hold your horses, Gabriel Q!

Did he really want to pack up his cameras and leave the country? Leave Hallie? Sometimes his assignments took him places where a woman wasn't safe, where a wife wasn't welcome.

Wife? Why was he counting chickens? After all, he had known Hallie O'Brien less than two days.

Or had he?

Like a merry-go-round, his thoughts kept circling, never leaving the place of origin. According to Hallie, they'd met and loved each other a hundred years ago. Even though her justification was a convenient justification for him, too, he had to change that belief, convince her that focusing her energy on the present, possibly the future, was much more rewarding.

But first he had to find her.

The bathroom door gaped open. The kitchenette was empty. The vestibule light only emphasized the dark family room. He began striding toward the studio, but halted when he heard the muffled sounds of a woman weeping.

The costume alcove!

Hallie sat in the corner, hugging her knees to her chest, shuddering from the intensity of her sobs.

"What's wrong?" Gabe rushed forward and hunkered down. "Earlier . . . on the couch. . . . did I hurt you?"

She raised her tear-drenched eyes and shook her head. Then she pointed toward the easel.

He gazed incredulously at what looked like a child's finger painting. Thick-smeared red, orange and yellow swirls completely covered the canvas.

"I kept adding more paint and I couldn't make myself stop," she cried, hiding her face against her bare knees.

"It's . . . different."

"Don't be tactful, Gabe. It's awful." She jerked her chin up so fast that tears sprayed like rain. "Do you see the man and woman at the window?"

"What window?"

"You've got to look very closely, beyond the flames. There's the vague suggestion of a roofline."

Ah, the colorful swirls were flames! With this new perspective, Gabe approached the canvas. Just below the hazy roofline was a small, open window. Through the window, Gabe could see the silhouettes of a man with his arm extended, his hand fisted, and a woman who appeared to be falling backwards. The figures were so tiny, Gabe could be wrong. But he didn't think so. Because he knew the legend of the Cripple Creek fire.

In April, 1896, a bartender named Otto Floto had crossed the intersection of Myers and Third, walked into the Central Dance Hall, climbed stairs to the second floor, then entered a room furnished with a bed, a washstand, two chairs and a table. Waiting inside was Otto's lady friend. One historian said her name was Minta, another said Lettie. In any case, Otto had fought with Minta or Lettie. On top of the table was a kerosene stove. On top of the stove was a pot of squirrel stew. During their violent struggles, the woman had fallen against the table and knocked over the stove.

Cripple Creek's Central Dance Hall, along with most of the other structures, had been built with green lumber cut from nearby government land during the first gold bonanza of 1892. The lumber had subsequently dried and the structures were in a bad state of dilapidation. When the Central Dance Hall flared, other stores and houses caught like boxes of matchsticks.

Gabe had a sudden thought that almost knocked him off his feet. Could Lettie be a nickname for Scarlet? Was the woman in the window Lady Scarlet?

Kneeling directly in front of Hallie, Gabe told her about the fire, but kept the Lady Scarlet theory to himself. Why agitate Hallie further? She was already so upset, her gaspy gulps sounded as if a pillow smothered her face.

"Honey, calm down. Take a deep breath." Gabe shook her very gently. She released her knees and crumpled forward. Hot tears immediately soaked his jeans, all the way through to his thigh. "Okay, okay, shhhh," he crooned, stroking her back. "Okay, little love, I'm here. I'll always be here for you."

Finally, inevitably, her sobs became small shudders. Gabe

shifted position, sitting with his back against the wall. Then he settled Hallie across his lap. Her curls tickled his chin.

"Sorry," she murmured. "I haven't cried like that since Gabriel threw my scent against the wall and broke the bottle."

"Gabriel threw your scent against the wall?"

"Did I say Gabriel? I meant Neil. My brother. He was angry at something I said, so he reached for the first thing at hand. It just happened to be a bottle of expensive perfume, a birthday present."

"Which birthday, Hallie?"

"My sixteenth."

"What did you say to make Neil angry?"

"I don't remember."

Gabe remembered her plea to Gabriel. *Why do you hesitate? Is it because I'm pure?*

Had Gabriel, rather than her brother, been angry enough to throw her perfume, her *scent* against the wall? Had Knickers initiated a seduction? That would explain Gabriel's reaction. It would also mean that Hallie had been "trancing" since age sixteen.

Another thought occurred. "Hallie, how old were you when your great-grandmother died?"

"I was a little kid. Why?"

"Maybe your great-grandmother originally came from Colorado and bent your ear with Cripple Creek tales, including the fire. You subconsciously absorbed her stories and—"

"Granny Bea died in 1984. She was eighty-nine. You just told me the fire occurred in 1896. How could Granny Bea recall events that happened when she was still in nappies?"

Disregarding Hallie's use of the word nappies for diapers, Gabe said, "Maybe somebody told *her*."

"Impossible. Assuming Granny Bea even came from Colorado, she was adopted when she was twelve months old."

"Far-fetched, huh?"

"Very." Hallie heaved a deep, quivery sigh. "I've still got the blue devils."

"I have the perfect cure for that. Let's go back to bed and snuggle."

"That sounds nice, Gabe, but I used acrylic paint and it should be dry by now. I want to prime my canvas, get rid of the fire."

"You can't put out a fire by priming a canvas."

"I know, but I want to try. I've *got* to try."

Suddenly, Gabe remembered Joe's Elk Creek casino ghost.

Was Knickers the little girl who had been abandoned during the Cripple Creek fire?

Chapter Seventeen

The next morning dawned autumn crisp, neither too hot nor too cold. Peering at the sky through the studio window, Hallie saw slivers of sunshine dancing up a storm. Half-hidden by clouds, the yellowish ballerinas wore gauzy tutus. But soon those peekaboo clouds would thicken, and . . .

Rain, rain, go away, Mary Knickers wants to play.

This time Hallie listened to the voice inside her head.

Mary Knickers? Holy Moses! The little girl's given name was Mary.

Hallie recalled her image when Marianne had gone into labor—a child clad in knickers, starting a fire in a cookstove. She also remembered that, as a little girl, she had often shed her clothes, leaving nothing more than underpants. If she hadn't been fiercely protected by her big brother, would the other kids have nicknamed her Panties or Undies?

"Hello, little love." Gabe entered the studio. "Did this morning's snuggle banish those blue devils?"

"Completely." She felt her cheeks bake. "How can I have devils, blue or otherwise, when you carry me off to heaven?"

"Hallie, you're adorable." Gabe righted the couch, then grinned ruefully at the teddy bear. Scooping it up, he placed it among his other props. "What would you like to do today? Sightsee?"

"Might we try Cripple Creek again?"

"No!" As if he regretted his sharp one-word outburst, he said, "Let's save Cripple Creek for Sunday. I've already made reservations at the Imperial Hotel and bought tickets for their famed melodrama."

"Sunday?" She walked over to the window. "That doesn't give me much time."

"For what?" Gabe asked.

Solving the puzzle, she thought. "Exploring Cripple Creek," she said, making an about-face. "I'm leaving Monday."

"Couldn't you stay longer?"

"Do you want me to stay?"

"Need you ask?"

Walking forward, Gabe tilted her chin and bestowed a kiss on her lips, still slightly swollen from this morning's activities.

"Yes, I want you to stay," he said.

"I think the little girl's given name was Mary," Hallie blurted, avoiding a commitment.

To stay or not to stay, she thought, paraphrasing Shakespeare. And wouldn't that be an awesome name for their first-born? William Shakespeare Quinn. Billy Q.

Why was she counting chickens before they hatched? Gabe hadn't said anything about marriage, and she was glad he hadn't. To wed or not to wed was a much more difficult decision than to stay or not to stay. What about her family back east? What about her career?

Horsefeathers! She could paint in Colorado. But would she continue painting Cripple Creek scenes? Gabriel? Lady Scarlet? Knickers? *Mary* Knickers?

"I think the little girl's given name was Mary," she said again.

"Hallie, let's forget the past and just enjoy the day. I'll take you sightseeing. You can play tourist. Throw on some jeans and a heavy sweater, lace up your sneakers, and we'll start with the Garden of the Gods."

"Garden of the Gods? Oh, I love that."

"As an artist, you'll love the red rocks."

"Do they tickle God's feet?"

"No," Gabe said. "They tickle one's fancy. There's a legend about the name. Two men surveyed the glorious scene. One said, 'Don't you think that this would be a great place for a Milwaukee beer garden?' 'Beer garden?' the other man said indignantly. 'Why, this is fit for a Garden of the Gods!' Maybe you should bring a sketch pad, honey. Or do you paint from memory?"

"Hah! You *do* think I paint from my memories."

"No, I don't. The question slipped out."

"Until recently, I worked from sketches or photos. Which reminds me. Would it take you very long to develop your pictures from yesterday?"

"No. Why?"

"The glen was so beautiful. The aspen leaves shimmered like a gold lamé gown, sprinkled with sequins. I'm not positive I could duplicate the color, but I'd like to try."

Hallie sounded sincere, yet Gabe suspected that she wanted to probe his photos very carefully, perhaps even discover the misty outlines of a cabin, a corral, and a rope clothespinned with knickers.

Knickers. *Mary* Knickers. The past was rapidly encroaching on the present, destroying the future, and Gabe felt a sorrowful ache in his gut.

Chapter Eighteen

Forget the past!

Gabe had told her to forget the past.

Hallie stared up at the skylight. Why couldn't she sleep? She wanted to sleep. Every bone in her body ached from exhaustion. Her head ached, too.

Holding both palms against her pounding temples, she pondered today.

Correction. Yesterday. It had to be long past midnight.

First, she and Gabe had toured the Garden of the Gods. He had laughingly called the precariously balanced rock formations "a supernatural catastrophe." But she thought the uplifted sandstone slabs looked more like mystic confections. There were even legendary names for the rocks: "The Angry Dolphin," "The Eagle with Pinions Spread." And her favorite, "Elephant Attacking a Lion."

Then they had walked through the Cheyenne Mountain Zoo, up and down twisty trails, pausing briefly so that Gabe could shoot pictures and rest his bad leg. Which, he said, felt fine. Just before leaving, she had bought Cheyenne Mountain Zoo T-shirts for her whole family, including tiny Shania.

While rain spit and sprinkled, she and Gabe ate a late lunch inside the famous Broadmoor Hotel, and he talked about the hotel's first annual bathing beauty contest, held in 1925. The girls had been shockingly attired in skimpy black suits with abbreviated skirts and black stockings.

Gabe's strong features had assumed mock-horror as he whispered that the stockings had been *rolled at the knees!*

After lunch, the rain stopped, as if God had plugged up the drain in a vast, porcelain sea of clouds. Gabe phoned Josh, who said that he planned a special candlelight dinner for Kayla.

Not wanting to intrude, yet agreeing that candlelight dining sounded like a fine scheme, Gabe had grocery shopped for wine, cheese, a loaf of crusty French bread, and candles. Just like a little kid, she had ridden the supermarket cart as they whizzed down the aisles. At the top of his lungs, Gabe had sung, "I want you to be my teddy bear," and her cheeks had turned as red as a stoplight.

Then Gabe had developed his roll of film.

"I see something strange in the background," Hallie had said. Gabe's gray-green eyes looked anxious, so she quickly added, "I see girls shockingly attired in skimpy black bathing suits with silk stockings rolled at the knees."

"Don't *do* that," he said.

She said, "Did you honestly think I might see Gabriel's cabin?"

"I think you wanted to see it."

"I'd rather see a cabin than a fire—"

"The fire was in your painting!"

"—because I was so happy at the cabin."

"Hallie, stop it! You weren't happy. Knickers was."

"Mary Knickers!"

"I don't care if she was called Mary Knickers or Shirley Temple Knickers. Did you know that Shirley Temple once visited the Broadmoor Hotel?"

"Hunky-dory!"

"Please, Hallie, forget the past."

"The past brought us together."

"No, it didn't. I'm not Gabriel."

"I only meant," she said, "that without my paintings we might never have met."

"Okay. I'm sorry. Let's tote our tired bodies into the bedroom, light the candles, then share some bread, cheese and wine."

"I'd rather share kisses, Gabe. Kisses are sweeter than wine."

Hallie had the strangest feeling she'd said that before. Granted, it sounded like a line from a popular song. However, long before the song had been sung, she had said, "I'd rather share kisses, Gabriel."

Gabriel, not Gabe!

Forget the past!

But it was hard to forget the past, especially when one's fingers curled around an imaginary paintbrush.

With an effort, she stiffened her hand. From the skylight, diluted moonlight shone down upon her taut knuckles. Terror stabbed through her as she watched her fingers convolute again. Her nails gashed her palm, and she felt a sorrowful ache in the pit of her stomach.

Chapter Nineteen

At first it looked like a parade.

Then, as more details evolved, a funeral procession.

A young girl—the bullfight girl—marched alongside the hearse, which held a lavender casket draped with crimson and white roses. The girl's dark red curls were pinned up, subdued by a straw boater. In her arms she held a baby. The baby wore two caps, one that hugged its head, one with a frilly bonnet's brim. Plump legs extended from the baby's white dress and straddled the young girl's waist.

A rider-less black stallion followed the funeral wagon. Atop his saddle lay a cross of pink carnations.

Heavily veiled women, hollow-eyed miners, and children of all ages lined the streets. Most faces were blurred. However, a few meticulously rendered expressions suggested sorrow. And curiosity. One sidewalk child bounced a ball. A second played with a monkey on a stick.

Hallie smelled the cloying fragrance of roses and carnations, but paint dominated all other smells. Having worked rapidly, wielding her brush like a pinwheel, her T-shirt and shorts reeked from the spill of acrylic oils and paint thinner.

"Honey?" Gabe swallowed a yawn as he advanced through the alcove's open doorway. "Again?"

"Please go back to bed," she insisted.

"Not unless you come with me."

"The smell." She bent over double. "It's making me sick."

Gabe raced forward, circled Hallie's waist, and immediately felt her oven-like heat. "Honey," he said, trying to modulate his voice, "you're burning up."

"That can't be true, Gabe. I'm so cold."

"Bed! Now! You need aspirin and—"

"I can't stand the smell!" Wrenching free, she bolted from the costume alcove and raced down the hall toward the bathroom.

Gabe had often helped medics tend wounded soldiers, so the sight of a sick woman didn't faze him. Quickly, efficiently, he soaked a washcloth with cold water and held it against her brow.

"Sorry," she gasped, sitting on her heels. Then, with a strangled cry, she bent forward again.

After a while, she looked up at him, her eyes unfocused.

"Sorry, Gabriel," she said, her voice sluggish. "I didn't mean to whoops, but I was so scared. Madam and the girls were in church. I left church and ran home because Mama Scarlet didn't feel good this morning. When she saw me she said she'd spank my be-hind, but before she could she grabbed her belly and let out a scream. She said to boil water. I washed the sweat from her face and I let her squeeze my hand and I sang a hymn, 'There Is Sunshine in my Soul.' I guess the baby slid out, but it seemed to pop out. Like a jack-in-the-box. Mama said to cut the baby's cord with a kitchen knife boiled in water, but I couldn't move because my legs were shaking so bad. I put my baby sister on Mama's belly. Then you showed up and cut the cord, so I don't know why my tummy hurts, but it does."

Feeling utterly helpless, Gabe watched Hallie glance down at the tiles. Then, very slowly, she raised her chin, and he saw that her eyes were still glazed over. This time, however, they were almost black with anguish.

"I saved Mama Scarlet when my baby sister was born," she cried, "but I couldn't save her from a broken heart. Why did my daddy come back?"

Rising, she grasped the sink for support. "He wasn't et by a bear. Mama Scarlet fibbed 'bout that. My daddy worked on a boat that traveled all over the world. When he came back he stayed with us, but he couldn't settle down. At the same time Mama birthed my baby sister, my daddy was out riding, hurdling fences, falling on his head, breaking his neck. Mama Scarlet always expected him to come back. Always. She had *hope.* She gave her body to the miners, but she never gave her soul. After my daddy passed, Mama Scarlet lived one year, twelve short months. She knew she was gonna die. She *willed* herself to die. It wasn't the fever that carried her away. It was a broken heart."

"Let me carry you to bed, Hallie," Gabe said. "No arguments, okay?"

He wished she would argue, or at least squirm a little. But she just lay in his arms, limp as a rag doll.

Somehow, Gabe persuaded the doctor to make a house call. Maybe it was the power of his name, Gabriel Q, which he used shamelessly. Maybe it was the mention of Jenn's father, still a vital force in Denver politics.

Gabe didn't want to drive Hallie to a hospital. He didn't want her sedated. He kept hearing the echo of her words: *I'm afraid I might never wake up . . . never wake up . . . never wake up . . .*

"Twenty-four-hour flu," the doctor grumped, scribbling a prescription for an antibiotic. "Make sure she drinks plenty of liquids and call me if she gets any worse."

Gabe knew the doctor's service would carefully screen future calls, but he didn't care. The prescription was in his shirt pocket and Hallie would be fully recovered in twenty-four hours.

But it was forty-eight hours before her fever broke.

The fingers that caressed her brow were warm, gentle. Hallie struggled to raise her heavy eyelids, hoping to meet Gabe's gray-green gaze. Instead, she saw a Cripple Creek ghost. The ghost looked like Mama Scarlet. Boy oh boy, Joe and the other casino owners would sure get a kick out of this.

"You've had schooling," said the ghost, "and I've kept you from the profession. You're pure, Mary, and I want you to stay that way. Promise me you'll stay pure."

"I promise, but you're not gonna die, Mama. The doctor says the fever will break soon."

"Promise me . . . that you'll find a good home . . . for your sister."

"Please, Mama, you're not—"

"*Promise,* Mary."

"I promise."

Burying her face in the pillow, she felt her heart plummet. She could easily find a family for her beautiful baby sister, but she was fifteen, already grown. In fact, the Homestretch's Madam had insisted she take Mama Scarlet's place and tonight she would entertain her first gentleman. Before she took Mama Scarlet's place, before she "entertained" her first gentleman, Madam wanted her to sing at the saloon so the gents could get a good look at her.

"A teaser," Madam said with a cackle. "When you sing, you must poke your titties out and lift your skirts. If you sing real good and get the gents all fired up, we might snag ourselves a rich old goat."

"I don't feel much like singing," she cried, turning over onto her back.

"Of course you don't," soothed a man, his voice tender. He sounded familiar.

Gabriel? No, not Gabriel.

Her vision blurred, then cleared, and she saw the saloon's interior. Gabriel played a game of poker and he had just made a wager.

"Don't bet your horse, Gabriel," she cried. "You need your horse."

"She's delirious, Josh," said the man with the tender voice.

Madam laid her cards on the table and somebody shouted, "I'll be damned! She wasn't bluffing. A full house. Kings and threes."

"He weren't bluffing, neither," said another gent. "He's got a full house, too. Aces and sevens."

"Poor Knickers," said a pasty-faced woman with sparse yellow hair. "Gabriel's cabin ain't got mirrors. Guess that's 'cause his face would shatter glass. Knickers once stole my hair restorer," she added gleefully.

"I did not, you hatchet-faced harlot!"

"Don't call me hatchet faced, you bitch!"

"Shut up, Mollie!" Gabriel glared at the pasty-faced woman with the sparse yellow hair.

The man with the tender voice added his two cents. "Keep sponging her, Josh," he said, "while I fetch more broth."

She rode Gabriel's horse, her hands clutching Gabriel around his middle. Glancing up at the sky, catching snowflakes on her long thick lashes, she said, "I'm so cold."

She was cold inside, too. Was it true? Would Gabriel's face shatter glass? Six months ago his handsome face had been badly scarred during a mine explosion and he had lost his right leg at the knee. His father owned the mine. Gabriel had been learning the business from the ground up when the explosion occurred. His father wanted him to come home to Denver, but Gabriel continued living in his small mountain cabin.

"I can't tolerate my family's sympathy or my fiancée's sacrificial attitude," he had told the parlor girls while he painted their portraits. The girls didn't care if he was scarred since he made *them* look so beautiful. She wasn't sure what sacrificial attitude meant, but she thought it might mean that Gabriel's snooty fiancée didn't love him anymore.

"I'm so cold," she repeated.

Someone wrapped a quilt around her and poured broth down her throat. She wanted to spit it up but Mama Scarlet said that spitting was bad etiquette.

Had she cooked the soup? She cooked for Gabriel and washed his clothes and kept his cabin clean and posed for his paintings. One night she crept into his bed and they canoodled. Half-asleep, Gabriel kissed her. Then he stopped. When she begged him to go on, he threw her bottle of scent against the wall. He said she was a child.

Bilgewater! She was sixteen, and her body had become a woman's body. She wasn't pretty, not by a long shot, but Gabriel made her feel pretty. In his paintings, her waist was pinched and her hips nicely rounded. In his paintings, her hair looked like a fox's tail rather than ripe strawberries.

The heat was unbearable. She thrashed about to escape it, kicking away at the blankets.

"Josh, she's burning up again," said the man with the tender voice, only now his voice sounded tearful.

Gabriel removed her wedding gown, then her white camisole and lacy drawers. His caresses seared her bare flesh, sending heat waves to the secret place between her legs.

She wanted him so badly. After two years, she didn't even see his scars. Anyway, it didn't matter if his face was scarred.

His lips and tongue worked just fine. And the loss of his leg had nothing to do with that special part of his body that brought her, first a stabbing pain, then unbearable pleasure. The pleasure far outweighed the pain. And, he said, she'd never experience pain again. Which was good, because she wanted to experience pleasure every night for the rest of her life.

She had always known that Gabriel loved her. Always.

When he told his parents about their marriage, they disinherited him. His wife was the daughter of a whore, they said.

Gabriel couldn't care less about being disinherited. He hunted game while she tended her vegetable patch. They had food and shelter and she felt happy, cherished, loved.

"She feels cooler," a man murmured.

"Thank God," said the man with the tender, tearful voice. "I don't know what I would have done, Josh. You see, I love her so much."

She and Gabriel rode toward their special glen. This time the aspen leaves shimmered and the autumn sun shone and she was neither too hot nor too cold.

Well, she was hot inside. Because she knew they would soon make love underneath their favorite tree. Afterwards, Gabriel must get back to work. Collectors were clamoring for his canvases. Gabriel might even become rich, a funny thought. What did rich feel like? Fat? Starched? Snooty?

Gabriel always shared his paint and brushes. The first time, wanting to please him, she had stared at an empty canvas, face-high, propped against wooden spokes. Then she had begun sketching a picture with charcoal. She filled in the lines and spaces and Gabriel taught her how to paint shadows.

She painted her baby sister, Beatrice, and all the pets she had cared for during her years at the Homestretch, and she painted Mama Scarlet.

"Now Mama Scarlet will live forever," she told Gabriel.

"So will you," he said.

Painting her portrait, he signed it with his first name but didn't add his last name. He didn't want to use the family name, he said. Not because he was *ashamed* of it, but because his father didn't *deserve* to have his name preserved. That was the only time Gabriel had ever sounded bitter about his disinheritance.

She understood why he felt so bitter. She never painted her daddy. Oh, he hadn't disinherited her, but if her daddy hadn't come back, Mama Scarlet would still be alive.

Her daddy and mama were buried next to each other, never to be separated again. Sometimes she thought she saw them, hand in hand, exploring the mountains, happy ghosts.

Gabriel's horse galloped faster and faster.

Hallie felt a cool breeze caress her cheeks. Squeezing her eyes shut, she fell into a deep, dreamless sleep.

Chapter Twenty

Hallie raised herself up on one elbow, wincing at the slight movement. Her body felt bruised. Had she fallen down the stairs? Turning her head, her puzzled gaze lit upon a basin and towel, situated next to a small vial of prescription pills. Her nightgown smelled like fabric softener. Her sheets smelled clean, too. How on earth could Gabe strip the mattress and wash the sheets while she slept?

She sniffed again and smelled . . . dog.

Which meant that Napkin had been here.

Featherbrained mooncalf! Josh had been here and left a lingering trace of St. Bernard. That made sense. Dog hairs probably clung to his clothes and . . . what the heck was Josh doing in Gabe's bedroom?

She moved her legs over the edge of the bed, dismayed by her lack of strength. In this new position, she could see that there was a banner thumbtacked to the wall. Large printed letters proclaimed: WELCOME BACK.

"Welcome back? Where did I go?"

"You took a journey through the past," said Gabe.

Startled by the sound of his voice, she saw him standing just inside the doorway. He carried a steaming bowl of something. Soup? Stew?

She glanced up at the skylight.

"The sun's so high, it must be noon or later," she said. "Holy Moses, Gabe, I slept round the clock."

"Honey, it's Friday."

"Friday?" She felt the color drain from her face.

Gabe placed the bowl on top of the bureau and raced toward the bed. "Take it easy, Hallie." Sitting next to her on the edge of the bed, he stroked the tangled curls away from her forehead.

She recalled her fevered musings. "They *were* lovers, Gabriel and Knickers."

"They were married."

"You can't be married and lovers at the same time?"

"Of course you can. I only meant—"

"Ohmigod, Gabe. Did I talk out loud?"

"Yup."

"The whole story?"

"Bits and pieces. You can fill in the blanks."

Hallie told him everything she remembered while he gently massaged her shoulders.

"I guess they lived happily ever after," she concluded. "No, they didn't. Otherwise, I wouldn't have felt my heart stop when I walked down Myers Avenue."

"Maybe you experienced a premonition, Hallie. Myers Avenue was the scene of the fire. And, years later, Scarlet's funeral."

"The comet!"

"What?"

"Why did I paint a comet?"

"Because there was a comet. It appeared in 1910."

"But what does the comet have to do with anything?"

"What does the Midland Terminal Railroad have to do with anything?"

"It led me to Cripple Creek. All my paintings are clues, Gabe."

"Let's see what you paint next, Hallie. Okay? I think the worst is over. Gabriel and Knickers were happily married. I'll bet your next few paintings show kids and cats and dogs."

"Speaking of dogs, what was Josh doing here?" Tentatively, she toed the carpet, then stood and stretched.

"Josh kept you company while I fetched the medicine and cooked . . ." Gabe paused, his gray-green eyes dancing. "*Brewed* chicken soup."

"I wasn't in any danger."

"Yes, you were. I was afraid . . ." Again, he paused.

"You were afraid I might go into a trance and not come out of it? Don't be silly. Now that I've found you, I plan to experience pleasure every night for the rest of my—"

"Life?"

"Visit." She felt a blush stain her cheekbones. Lowering her lashes, she buried her gaze in the basin.

"Hallie, you're adorable."

"I'm adorably hungry."

"You vant to eat my heart?"

"Basted frog! You sound like I sing. Don't ever try to audition for a theatrical production of *Dracula*. Stop laughing, you idiot. I need real food, the kind you chew, but first I need a real bath."

"Perhaps you might care to taste a different portion of my anatomy." Glancing down at his lower body, he quirked an eyebrow. "I know vampires suck blood, but I don't believe they, um, reproduce."

"I need a bath, Drac. Preferably, a bubble bath."

"Okay."

"You have bubbles?"

Rising from the bed, weaving his fingers through hers, he led her toward the bathroom. "Choose your scent, Hallie. Apple, lilac, clouds—"

"Wait a sec. What do clouds smell like?"

"Angel wings."

"You're nuts."

"I bought a plastic bottle of clouds because I read somewhere that it's Mel Gibson's favorite."

She watched Gabe plug up the drain, turn on the faucets, then rummage in the cabinet beneath the sink.

"Damn," he said, "I'm all out of clouds. We'll have to use this pink stuff."

"What do you mean, we?"

"Would you deny me a bath, Hallie?"

"No. It's your tub."

"Our tub."

Dubiously, she studied the antique tub with its four claw feet and shower fixture. The pink stuff had bubbled and the bathroom smelled like Marianne's raspberry lemonade.

"Take off your nightgown," Gabe urged, "before the water cools."

"You first, Drac. You're over six feet tall so you'll have to bend your knees."

"I plan to bend my knees over your prone body. Hurry, Hallie. We're losing the bubbles." He grinned wickedly. "Alice W. O'Brien's a bullyragged jellyfish," he taunted.

"I'm no coward!" She shed her nightie, then sank down into the water so that her toes were near the drain, beneath the faucets. "Okay, Gabe, you can stick your butt in the air. I was trying to be nice."

"You have a nice butt."

"How can you tell? It's squashed against the bottom of the tub."

Gabe grinned like an idiot. Bubbles formed a halo around Hallie's dark curls and a white goatee accentuated her chin. More bubbles hid the tantalizing curves of her body. He wanted to keep the conversation lighthearted, but he knew that anything he said would have a raspy-throated quality.

"Jellyfish got your tongue?" she taunted.

Damn, was she totally unaware of her seductive powers? How could she help but become aware when he removed his jeans? His erection would surely betray his desire.

The bubbles were soapy, he reminded himself, even though they looked like carbonated fizz. So he'd drain the tub, watch the bubbles disperse, then add fresh water before tasting her raspberry-scented flesh.

Hallie's eyes widened as Gabe kicked his jeans free from his long, muscular legs. How could a man swell so fast without kissing? Without even touching? On the other hand, she hadn't kissed or touched him, and yet she felt her nipples swell. Maybe ache would be a better word. No. They swelled.

Perhaps the word for Gabe was tumefy. She had once read that word in a book and looked it up. The dictionary didn't have tumefy, but it did have tumescence, a readiness for sexual activity marked by excessive fullness of the sex organ.

What a great word, tumescence. Rather like luminescence. Hallie felt luminous and . . . why was Gabe draining the water?

"Please don't drain the water, Gabe. I need a long soak. I feel fine, honest . . ." Her plea subsided when he climbed into the tub.

"I thought you might taste like soap," he explained, "so I'm draining the bubbles."

"You vant to eat my heart?"

"Your heart's a good place to start." On his knees, he adjusted the faucets. Then he flipped the little gizmo that controlled the showerhead.

"You'll soak the bathroom floor," she gasped.

"Downstairs I have a mop. Under the bathroom sink I have sponges. Your call."

"If you're not careful, I'll call your *bluff.*"

"I'll be very careful." Concentrating on every sensual

curve, Gabe traced the arc of Hallie's graceful neck, the tilt of her small but surprisingly full breasts, the indentation of her slender waist, the flare of her hips.

"You're right," he said.

"About what?"

"You should be on top."

He shifted their positions so that her back rested against his drawn-up knees. Spray from the showerhead pelted them mercilessly, washing away every vestige of bubbly soap. Now he could taste. Now he could play Dracula.

Except . . . why suck blood when he could suck nipple?

Hallie ignored the spray that rebounded off her shoulders. With a moan, she inched forward and felt Gabe penetrate. Funny. She had always believed that a man must be on top so that his sex organ could slant downwards, between a woman's spread thighs. It had never occurred to her that his organ could sustain an upward slant. Actually, she thought with a blush, Gabe's organ had no slant at all.

Her body spasmed and she reached out blindly, trying to get a firm grip on his shoulders. But his rippling muscles were wet, slick. In any case, she had lost all control, sinking backwards toward his bent knees.

He had no trouble grasping her waist, then lifting her up and down, up and down. Each time, he felt firmer, more substantial. How was that possible? He had begun this unique love lesson already . . . tumefied.

Her spasms became explosive bursts, as if she'd swallowed nitroglycerin. Gabe swallowed her happy sobs, but his kisses were even more inflammatory. Eyes shut, she felt him cradle her back as she sank toward his knees again. Rocking from side to side, she inhaled spray.

"Don't look up," he said. "Sorry . . . I should have turned off the shower. Too late now."

She felt a new wetness, and a primitive satisfaction at her power to cause that wetness. Then Gabe cried out, and she cried out, and she saw a rainbow, even though she was vaguely aware that she viewed the rainbow through tap water, not rain.

Later, dryer, they nestled . . . *canoodled* together in bed.

"I think I've found another laughin' place," Hallie said. "Who'd have thought it would be an antique bathtub?"

Then she had to explain about B'rer Alice, adapted from Uncle Remus and B'rer Rabbit.

"Everybody's got a laughin' place," she said. "What's yours, Gabe?"

"I thought it was traipsing all over the world, shooting photos. Then I thought it was developing pictures in my own darkroom." He sighed a contented sigh. "But now, Alice W. O'Brien, it's anyplace *you* are. There's only one thing that would make my laughing place perfect."

"And that thing is?"

"I want to know what the 'W' in Alice W. stands for."

She laughed so hard she couldn't tell him.

Chapter Twenty-One

Gabe knew that, eventually, he'd have to rise and prepare something to eat. The soup on the bureau was ice-cold. They had skipped breakfast and lunch. If this continued, he and Hallie would love each other as ghosts. Skinny ghosts.

As if she'd read his mind, she said, "I'm hungry, but I don't feel like moving. Is there a take-out service that delivers food to the bedrooms of starved, satiated lovers?"

"Yup. It's called Joshua Quinn."

"Don't you dare call Josh, you basted frog."

"Basted frog?" He picked up her right hand and pressed it against his lips before cradling it in his own hands, working the fine bones gently. "I've improved a lot since the fifth grade. When we were in the bathtub, my kisses almost drowned you."

"Very funny." She freed her fingers so that she could frame his face. "I guess a few weeks, months, even years of Charles-passion are worth the risk."

"Charles? Charles who?"

"Bronson."

"You've lost me, honey."

"In his movies, Bronson's lover always dies."

"From passion?"

"No. Assassins."

"I'll protect you from assassins."

"And sunsets?"

"Yup."

"Thanks, Drac." She chewed her bottom lip. "How about comets?"

"If a comet should appear, which is virtually impossible, we'll share the sight together."

"Comets scare me, Gabriel. Did you know that the miners won't work because they don't want to die underground? Quite a few went home to spend their last days with their families. I saw a newspaper story inside Harper's Grocery. Mark Twain said he came in with Halley's Comet and expected to go out with it. Mr. Harper told me about this vender selling comet pills outside the Imperial Hotel. The pills are supposed to protect people from the comet's dire effects. Could we buy some pills, Gabriel? Please?"

"Hallie!"

"Oh, God." She shook her head, as if to clear away spiderwebs. "I don't know why I just said that, Gabe, honest I don't. I wasn't trancing. The words just popped out."

After a long silence, he said, "Mark Twain died in 1910."

"I didn't know that. You're so smart." Obviously hoping he'd ignore the rest of her outburst, she caressed his jawline.

If I'm so smart, why can't I solve the mystery of Gabriel and Knickers? Gabe thought.

Tenderly, he ran his fingers through Hallie's curls, as if answers were hidden amongst the thick, dark strands. But one big question kept repeating itself, over and over again. Were her fevered dreams real, or merely fevered dreams?

The last thing Gabe meant to do was fall asleep. But Hallie's hands had abandoned his face to massage the tight muscles in his shoulders and back, then his arms and legs, until even his toes were beyond the power of motion. He started to say "I love you" but "I love" was as far as he got before he curled on his side and darkness closed over him.

★ ★ ★ ★ ★

Hallie watched Gabe sleep. It was only fair. After all, he had spent endless hours watching her. Finally, she settled against him, reveling in the fit of her back against his chest, her butt against his stomach, as if they had always belonged to each other. Not just a hundred years ago. Always.

Maybe she had been Cleopatra and Gabe her Marc Anthony. Maybe he had been a swarthy pirate and she had played his innocent hostage. Maybe she had been a spinning wheel–drugged princess and Gabe her handsome prince, waking her with a deep, tongue-thrusting kiss.

She and Gabe awoke before sunset to touch each other in wordless delight, and she was Hallie, and Gabe was Gabe, and that was the way they both wanted it.

Always.

Chapter Twenty-Two

Gabe's arms and legs were moist.

His fingers opened, releasing the ball. His racket drew back, then whipped through the air, its impact against the ball reverberating in the early morning's stillness.

Except for a few Disney *Dumbo* crows, balanced precariously on nearby telephone wires, the courts were vacant, as if they'd been jilted by tennis lovers.

Hallie was hard-pressed to return Gabe's serve. Stretching her strength to the limit, she almost performed a split in her eagerness to backhand the ball. With satisfaction, she saw it drift across the net, not far from the sidelines.

Gabe raced forward, then watched the ball bounce twice. "Out of bounds?" he asked, his voice mock-hopeful.

"You wish!" Covertly, Hallie admired the way his white shirt clung to his chest and abdomen, outlining the muscles beneath. His hip bones pressed against his blue shorts. He was fatless and faultless. Well, maybe not faultless. He had double-faulted on more than one serve. "I win the match, Drac, six–three."

"Knock off the Drac, Hallie. Vampires don't play tennis in brilliant sunlight." He grinned ruefully. "Did you let me win that last game on purpose?"

"No way! You're very good."

"I'm out of practice. That's not an excuse," he hastened to add. "It's just that I haven't picked up a racket since . . ." He glanced down at his leg. "My knee feels a little stiff, but I think I can last through one more match. How do *you* feel?"

"Fit as a fiddle. I wonder why they always say that. I mean, why is a fiddle more fit than any other instrument? Why can't someone be fit as a flute?"

Hallie's laughter sounded like the trill of a flute, Gabe thought. His gaze traveled from her flickering dimple to her faded yellow button-down shirt, which she said was her brother Neil's and which was much too large for her. The shirttails were tied in front, emphasizing her flat stomach and a small waist that disappeared into white shorts, only to emerge below, beautifully transformed into a pair of legs that were firm at the thighs, firm at the calves, and—despite her bulky white socks—delicate at the ankles. She wore white sneakers and she made sneakers look sexier than high heels.

"Are you hungry?" he blurted, trying to erase the image of Hallie in high heels, only heels, nothing else.

"Gabe, I ate enough last night to sink a ship."

"That was last night. We've metabolized since then."

Her cheekbones turned a lovely shade of crimson, as if she were visualizing their predawn, metabolizable workout. "Okay," she said. "After I whip your butt in the next game, we can share a humongous brunch. Winner pays."

"Deal. Even though I think you're really Monica Seles."

She implored the sky, then said, "Monica could whip *my* butt with one hand tied behind her back, and she uses both hands to swing her racket."

"So do you."

As he toed the white line, Gabe remembered Hallie's swinging motion when he'd cradled her body inside the bathtub. She had surrendered to him completely, or maybe it was the other way around. Either way, he suddenly wanted to be with her in the tub again, rather than facing her across a sea of mesh-webbed net.

On the other hand, he liked this fiercely competitive Hallie. She clutched her racket tightly, waiting for his serve. Her dark curls shimmered and her dark brown eyes squinted against the sun's glare. Right now her face was tense with purpose, but she had the best laughter he'd ever heard. Just listening to it made him happy. Hallie didn't have *a* laughing place. She *was* a laughing place.

A sudden cloud hid the sun as Gabe remembered that B'rer Rabbit had led Br'er Fox down the garden path. Because B'rer Rabbit's laughin' place was a tangled cluster of needle-sharp thorns.

He shook his head at the fanciful notion, and, as the sun exited the cloud, he resumed his appraisal of Hallie.

When she wasn't trancing, she was comfortable to be with. She seemed competent in just about everything she did, but her independence didn't cost her one shred of femininity.

Her lithe body, however, was costing him more than a shred of concentration. Arching his back, he hit the ball as hard as he could.

Distracted by a man and woman walking toward them, Hallie hit a lob that floated lazily through the air. Gabe skipped in place, following the arc of the ball, his right arm suspended. This would be an easy point. *Fifteen–love, my love,* he thought.

A woman's voice shouted, "Gabriel Q! I can't believe it!"

Startled, Gabe hesitated, and now the ball was too low. He knew he should let it bounce. Instead, he swung, catching it on the wood of his racket. The ball landed safely across the net, but Hallie sprang forward. The thrust of her racket whooshed through the air, and Gabe could only watch as the blur that had once been a ball caught the corner of his back court.

"Love–fifteen," he said. Then, with an effort, he stretched his mouth into a smile of acknowledgment. "Hi, Jenn."

"Hello, Gabe." She flounced toward him, her short tennis skirt flipping with every flounce. "This is the last place I ever expected to find *you.*"

"Why? We've played here before and I've kept my membership dues up-to-date."

"Darling, we haven't played tennis since your patriotic accident."

"Dammit, Jenn, my accident wasn't patriotic. I just happened to be standing in the wrong place at the wrong time."

Unable to resist, he performed a couple of deep knee bends and was sorely tempted to kick out like a Russian folk dancer.

"As you can plainly see," he continued, "I'm on my way to a full recovery. You should have waited a few more days before breaking off our engagement."

Hallie had circled the net and was walking toward Gabe and the gorgeous woman who resembled Joshua Quinn's Beauty. Now she halted, her breath catching in her throat. Engagement? Gabe had neglected to mention that little fact.

In fact, she knew very little about his personal life.

I know more about Knickers and Gabriel.

Bilgewater! She knew that Gabe was infinitely tender and compassionate and dependable, and she loved him.

After all, he was her dream man, her perfect man.

Gabe watched Jenn beckon toward a heavily bearded guy whose mesh tank top and ragged cutoffs displayed a set of bulging muscles.

"Cyclone darling," she cooed, "I'd like you to meet my fiancé."

"Ex-fiancé," Gabe muttered.

"Gabe darling, this is Gusty Cyclone, the wrestler," she said, ignoring Gabe's modification. "Most people call him 'The Wasp.' "

"I float like a butterfly, sting like a bee," The Wasp bragged, tilting the brim of his Colorado Rockies baseball cap. "I didn't make that up myself," he added.

Gabe sincerely doubted the wrestler *could* float. Waiting until Hallie joined them, he said, "Jennifer Bernadette Dominger Greengart and, er, Wasp, this is Hallie O'Brien."

"The artist?"

"Jenn," Gabe said through clenched teeth, "why do you have to designate every name with a profession?"

Her eyes blazed, but she merely stroked The Wasp's bulging forearm.

"Cyclone darling," she said, "this scowly man is Gabriel Q, the famous *porn* photographer."

The Wasp's small eyes widened. "That's great, dude," he said. "I don't know nothin' 'bout cameras, but I'd sure like to see ya work, if ya get my drift."

Where on earth had Jenn found this lunkhead? Gabe wondered. And why was she wasting her time with him?

As if he'd read Gabe's mind, the lunkhead said, "Jenn here wants to teach me tennis. She says I ain't got no grace. But I say who needs grace when they hand over a six-figure check after every performance?"

Hallie said, "Performance?"

"I meant wrestling match, miss."

"Please walk Cyclone to the baseline and show him how to hold a racket, Gabe darling," Jenn said, her voice a plea. "Pretty please? With sugar on top?"

Shading her eyes with one hand, Jennifer Bernadette Dominger Greengart watched Gabe stride toward the backcourt, The Wasp lumbering a few paces behind. Then she stared at Hallie. "Gabe and I had a little spat," she said, her voice sweet as sugar. "I tried to give him back his engagement ring but he insisted I keep it."

Hallie said, "When?"

"I beg your pardon?"

"When did you spat?"

"Last Saturday. When did you arrive?"

"Arrive?" Hallie decided to give Jennifer Bernadette et cetera a taste of her own medicine. "Oh, you mean *come*." She giggled. "Come, get it?"

"No, I don't get it. Aren't you Hallie O'Brien, the famous artist? Don't you live in New York?"

"Dang, that Gabe's such a kidder. Guess he thought he'd impress you with some big shot named Cally-fornia Brine, huh?"

"No, not California. Hallie. Hallie O'Brien, not Brine."

"Whatever." With her racket, Hallie nudged Jenn in the ribs. "My name's Michelle Bouche, Micki for short. Spelled M-i-c-k-i, not M-i-c-k-e-y, like the, you know, mouse."

"I . . . I beg your pardon?"

"Don't beg, dear, it lacks grace. I'm an artist, but I'm Micki Bouche, the famous striptease artist. Gabe shot me . . ." She giggled again. "Shot pictures of me last Monday. No, Tuesday. What's today? Friday? Saturday? It's so easy to lose track of time when you don't have a clock. I guess you can always glance up at the skylight, but that only tells you when it's day or night, not what time it is. Your face looks funny, Miss Greengart. Not funny funny. Funny strange."

"Skylight . . . no clock . . . you were in Gabe's bedroom!"

"Very good. You catch on quick." Hallie heaved a mock sigh. "Do I have to spell it out for you? Gabe clicked his camera and *we* clicked. He said I reminded him of his fiancée, his *ex*-fiancée, which is a hoot now that I've met you. We don't look anything alike."

"Cyclone darling," Jenn yelled, "let's get out of here!"

Hallie said, "Don't you want to play a game?"

"I thought we *were* playing games."

"I meant tennis, dear."

Jenn smoothed her short designer dress, a dress that might have given Venus Williams pause. Her index finger lingered at the embroidered WIMBLETON directly above her left breast. Then she stared disdainfully at Hallie's shirttails. "I'm afraid you wouldn't be much competition," she said with a sneer.

Hallie stifled a grin, knowing that England's famous tennis tournament was held at Wimble*don*, not Wimble*ton*.

"Maybe we could make the game more interesting," she said.

"Interesting?"

"Yes. We could wager. I'll wager my gramophone and horse against your knickers."

"Gramophone? Horse? Knickers? What the hell are you talking about?"

Damn, Hallie thought. Just like last night, in the bedroom with Gabe, the words had popped out.

"That was a joke, a private joke," she said, watching Gabe and The Wasp walk toward them. "I didn't mean your knickers, or panties, although I'm fairly certain I can whip the pants off you. I meant your engagement ring. I don't have an engagement ring . . . yet . . . but I'd be willing to bet its value in hard, cold cash."

"My diamond is very expensive, Ms. Bouche."

"So's my companionship. An artist can make a fortune . . ." She darted a glance toward The Wasp. "If you get my drift. Of course, I never charge Gabe. Do I, Gabe darling?"

"Charge me for what?"

"Never mind, you big ol' teddy bear. I've just made a fun suggestion . . . a wager. Your ex-fiancée's engagement ring against its cash value. And I do believe Jennifer Bernadette Dominger Greengart wants to play tennis."

"You *bet* I do! Clear the court!"

Gabe thought about voicing an objection, but realized any protest would be futile. Jenn's face, more often than not unmarred by passion, looked as if she'd donned a mask. Her mascara-drenched eyes were slits and her full, glossy, collagen-injected lips had thinned.

He knew, without a single doubt, that Hallie would never harm a fly. But she looked as if she wanted to pin a living, breathing butterfly to a corkboard.

Leading The Wasp toward the sidelines, Gabe tried to hide his anxiety. Jenn had been taking lessons from a pro since the age of ten while Hallie had just recovered from a serious illness. He didn't know Hallie's financial status, but Jenn's diamond had cost a pretty penny—many pretty pennies.

Hallie turned to Jenn. "Do you want to warm up, Miss Greengart?"

"No. I can beat you with one hand tied behind my back."

"Okay."

"I beg your pardon?"

"You can tie one hand behind your back."

"I wasn't serious, Ms. Bouche."

"Micki. Do you know what *bouche* means in French?"

"I never studied French."

"I did. It means mouth."

"You *do* have a big mouth."

"That's true. Gabe says I'm the wolf who ate *Mademoiselle*

Riding Hood. I told him the wolfette who eats *Monsieur* Riding Hood might be more apropros."

While Jenn stood there speechless, Hallie pinged a string with her fingernail, happy that she'd packed her own racket. It felt comfortable in her hand, an extension of her fingertips. She'd bought the racket at a charity sports auction, draining her bank account to outbid several collectors. The racket had once belonged to Martina Navratilova.

"Hey, Martina," Hallie murmured under her breath, turning away from Jenn. "I've been bothered by ghosts lately, but I could sure use your spiritual, if not physical, presence today. Jennifer Bernadette et cetera looks as if she might catch the ball with her teeth and spit it back."

Martina didn't answer, of course, but Hallie knew what Marianne would say. "Forget Jennifer Bernadette et cetera," Marianne would say. "Forget The Wasp. Forget Gabe. 'Sesame Street' 's Big Bird introduced a new C-word this morning. C for concentration."

You're right, Marianne, thanks!

Turning back to Jenn, Hallie said, "Shall we toss for the serve? On second thought, I'll serve. That'll give you a chance to warm up."

"I'm warm enough, thank you very much, so I'll serve first."

"Okay. In that case, I get to choose my side of the court."

Deliberately, Hallie stayed where she was, where Gabe had been during their last game, letting Jenn face the sun. Which now shone with a fierce, almost blinding brilliance.

Undaunted, Jenn strolled toward the sidelines and snatched The Wasp's baseball cap from his head. She placed the cap on her own streaky blonde hair, expertly styled in an upswept ducktail. The cap's brim shaded her eyes.

"Ready?" she said.

Without waiting for an answer, she served.

Second oldest trick in the book, thought Hallie, returning the serve.

Jenn smashed it back with all her strength, sending an apparent winner deep to Hallie's backhand. Streaking toward the ball, Hallie picked it up less than a foot off the ground, then drilled it straight down the line, past Jenn.

After that, the score seesawed. Both women played with a gritty determination and Hallie was beginning to regret her impulsive wager. Then Jenn served a curving ball that hooked short, just across the net, near the sideline. Damn, Hallie thought, barely able to return the serve. Now Jenn need only punch an easy volley safely down center court.

Instead, Jenn tried for a bedazzling touch-angle volley, missed, and lost the point.

Aha! There was another C-word. Confidence. Maybe it was an O-word. Overconfidence. Several spectators had joined Gabe and The Wasp, and Jenn couldn't resist the satisfaction of making difficult shots, aiming for the lines. She pictured herself as a seeded superstar, never realizing that genuine superstars didn't show off. Genuine—not Jenn-uine—superstars played to win.

With a tight smile, Hallie began setting up glamorous shots for overconfident Jenn to miss.

They had reached match point when Jenn served a flat, penetrating ball. She immediately rushed in behind it to the net. Hallie lobbed defensively, a proper lob that would land too deep for Jenn to smash an overhead winner. Turning, Jenn ran to the baseline and skipped in place near where the ball would land. Then she raised her racket-free hand and gestured toward the left corner of Hallie's court.

"That's where it's going to land, you overpriced stripper!" she shouted.

There was an audible gasp from the spectators as, still pointing to the left, Jenn blasted the ball toward the extreme right.

Oldest trick in the book, thought Hallie, as she sent a topspin backhand cross-court and watched it land a yard beyond Jenn's reach.

Jenn yelled, "Out!"

"In!" yelled the crowd.

"Gabe?" Jenn settled her liquid gaze on the man who had always satisfied her every whim. "You're standing near the line. Which was it, darling? Out or in?"

"In," he said.

Hallie approached the net, her hand extended.

Jenn gave it a quick shake. "Our bet was a joke, right?"

"Wrong."

"You really want my diamond?"

"*My* diamond."

"Okay. I'll send it . . . where? A whorehouse? Gabe's house? The gutter?"

"None of the above. You can mail it, with adequate insurance, to Bayside, New York. Josh has my address."

"But I thought . . ." Jenn's eyes narrowed. "You really *are* Hallie O'Brien, aren't you?"

"Yes. My stripper act was the joke."

Jenn shot a quick glance toward The Wasp, who was now standing a short distance away. He had flexed his upper arms and two giggly young women were hanging from his biceps.

Utterly defeated, Jenn said, "Good-bye, Gabe. Good luck, Ms. O'Brien."

Hallie pinged her racket's string. "I think you need luck more than I do, Ms. Greengart. They say diamonds are a girl's best friend and you look as if you just lost your best friend, so you can keep the ring. I don't need diamonds. I need answers."

Jenn's brow beetled. "Answers to what?"

Knickers and Gabriel, Hallie thought.

From the corner of her eye, she saw Gabe's expression. He looked as if he wanted to catch a tennis ball with his teeth and spit it back at her.

He had no right to look like that! Hallie felt her own anger churning, simmering, mighty close to a boil.

The man of her dreams had forgotten to mention two relevant pieces of information.

His engagement.

And his "little spat" with Jennifer Bernadette et cetera.

Maybe her perfect man wasn't so perfect, after all.

Chapter Twenty-Three

Hallie leaned against the TV. On its screen a young, non-seeded player was beating the logo-embroidered panties off a seeded player during the opening round of a nationally televised tennis tournament. Hallie uncharacteristically ignored the action. Instead, she watched Gabe pace up and down the family room, halting every so often to straighten a film poster that didn't need straightening. Even though he no longer perspired, his white shirt clung to the broad expanse of his chest every time he lifted his arms.

"Why did you tell Jenn to send the ring to New York?" he finally asked, halting mid-stride.

"Is that why you wouldn't utter one word during our drive home? Are you mad about the engagement ring?"

"No, not the ring."

"If you caught the whole conversation, Gabe, I told your fiancée she could keep it."

"My ex-fiancée, Hallie, and I don't give a damn if she puts the ring through her ear, her nose, or her nip—"

"I need a shower, Gabe. Badly. I'm stickier than a newly paved street. *You* might consider sticking your head beneath a cold water faucet. Perhaps you can wash away that hot streak under your collar."

"Why send the ring to New York, Hallie?"

"Because that's where I live. Remember?"

"And what was that damnfool wager all about? Were you jealous?"

"No. The wager was impulsive, Gabe *darling.* Your Jennifer Bernadette et cetera got *me* hot under the collar."

"She's not *my* Jennifer." With a flick of his wrist, Gabe turned off the TV. "Why send the ring to Bayside, Hallie?"

"I just told you. That's where I—"

"Live. Yes, I know. Didn't we talk about you staying longer, maybe even forever?"

"I . . . you . . . we never said forever."

"It was implied."

"It wasn't implied." She tried to remain calm, reasonable, curb her Irish temper, inherited from her Irish father, who didn't have a volatile bone in his body.

Gabe slapped the fireplace mantel. "Do you honestly believe I would make love to you, then send you home with a 'let's get together real soon, babe'?"

"Why not? It's the twenty-first century, Gabe, although the 1890s were probably worse. Especially in Colorado. Cripple Creek was a slam-bam-thank-you-ma'am kind of town, and Lady Scarlet's a prime example. She entertained gentlemen, including Mary Knickers's daddy, and they all left her flat. I've got a feeling they didn't even wave good-bye. Nobody believed that women of ill-repute had hearts and souls, much less emotions."

"Knickers's daddy came back."

"Bully for Knickers's daddy."

"And your slam-bam examples were whores, Hallie, not women of ill-repute. They didn't *entertain* gentlemen, they—"

"Knickers wasn't a whore!"

"And *you're* not Knickers!"

"At least the 1890s were honest, Gabe."

"What the hell does *that* mean?"

Walking away from the TV, Hallie straightened a poster he had tilted, reaching on tiptoe to align its frame. "If a man broke his engagement, he probably said something to the next woman on his list, something like, 'Oh, yeah, before I forget, my fiancée and I broke up.' "

"That's a bit modern for the nineteenth century, don't you think?"

"How about 'my intended and I terminated our relationship'?"

"The next woman on his list? Dammit, Hallie, you're not talking about the 1890s. You're talking about today."

"And the men were honest in other ways. When a girl was a well-bred lady, they courted her. If they needed . . . relief . . . they slept with a parlor girl. And they paid her for her time."

"Are you saying that you were my relief?"

"Yes. No. Let's try another R-word. Rebound. You and Jenn split last Saturday. Last Saturday, Gabe. One short week ago!"

"We split months ago, Hallie, only I wouldn't admit it." Cradling her chin with his hand, he stared into her eyes. "Do you want me to court you? I will. Do you want me to get down on my knees and beg your forgiveness for not mentioning my broken engagement? I will, gladly. I love you, Hallie. I've loved you from the first moment you fell into my arms. It wasn't your beauty, although you take my breath away. It was something deeper, something that hit me like a ton of bricks, something everlasting."

"Knickers and Gabriel felt that way."

"If you want to believe we were Knickers and Gabriel, I'll deal with it. But please don't think you're my relief. Or merely a rebound romance."

"I don't, Gabe, not really." On tiptoe again, she wound her arms around his neck and searched for the lips that took her breath away.

After a kiss that left her dizzy and disoriented and craving more, she heard him say, "Do you want me to court you?"

"No. I want you to love me."

"That's a fact, ma'am, not a request."

"Then you must entertain me, sir," she teased, her dark brown eyes sparkling with mischief.

"It would be my pleasure. But you have to pay."

"What's your price?"

"How much of my valuable time do you require?"

"A lifetime. Is that too long or too short?"

"Too short. However, we can negotiate. How about three bone-crushing hugs?"

"Wait, Gabe! Don't hug me!"

"You're supposed to hug *me*."

"It's the same thing, and I'm all sweaty. A sweat-drenched man smells manly, but a woman smells . . . sweaty."

"Hallie, you're adorable."

"Am I really?"

"Yup."

"Cross my heart," they both said together. Then, together, they reached for each other's hearts.

"Shower," she gasped, her palms pressed against his chest.

"I've got a much better idea." Twining her fingers through his, he led her toward the staircase. "Sponge bath."

"You have a sponge?"

"Several. They're beneath the bathroom sink, along with my bottles of Cloud Bubble Bath." He pushed her in front of him, his hands molding her backside. "Hurry, Hallie. A certain portion of my anatomy can't wait to watch me sponge you off."

"A 'certain portion of your anatomy' doesn't have eyes," she stated, her pragmatism rising to the surface.

"Then why," Gabe said, "is it responding with a salute?"

"Responding to what?"

"The sight of your butt wending its way up the stairs."

"Legs wend. A butt doesn't wend."

"Yours does. By the way, has anyone ever told you that you're a tad pragmatic?"

"Yes." She sighed. "Okay, I give up. Wend, salute, explode, I don't care. Let's just reach the bathroom so that you can sponge and I can see your so-called salute for myself."

"You don't have to see it. You can feel it." He nudged her backside.

"Holy Moses! Now it's sideways."

"Hallie, what on earth are you talking about?"

"Slants. Organs."

"A slanting organ?"

"Yes. No. Yes."

"Honey, do you mean a body part? Or a pipe organ?"

She felt her cheeks bake. "Why would I be talking about pipe organs?"

"Maybe you hear music."

"That comes later, after we explode. And the music is played by an orchestra, an imaginary orchestra, not one organ, although I suppose the organ could lead the orchestra like . . . like a baton."

"I'm getting all kinds of jumbled images, little love. In any case, your orchestra's not imaginary. I've heard it, too."

"Really?"

"Cross my heart."

"Have you heard voices, Gabe?"

"Sure. Your voice. My voice."

"I meant . . . never mind." Entering the bathroom, she reached for the tub faucets.

"Hold it, Hallie. I said sponges."

"You weren't kidding?"

"Why would I kid about an important thing like sponges?"

"But we'll get the floor wet. Again."

"When we build our dream house, we'll include a bathroom drain. Forget the tub. We'll slope the floor, drill a hole through the wall, and let the water *wend* its way outside."

A dream house meant a commitment, she thought. Maybe she'd better veer away from that subject. "Wow," she said. "I can see your salute now. It's pooching your shorts. Better take them off."

"Not so fast, honey. That's part of the fun."

Hallie felt her heart threaten to burst through her shirt. Gabe, rather than the antique tub, was her laughin' place.

Fun, he'd said. The overeager fingers and lips she'd endured, even Ivan's, especially Ivan's, had always been so painstakingly serious—as if the man had something to prove. Gabe had nothing to prove. He was more concerned with her pleasure than his, so he relaxed and let nature take its course. And if that course included a tickle or three, so much the better. Gabe was her laughin' place and love was laughter. Love was other things, as well, including an occasional tear and quarrel, but first and foremost it was laughter.

Laughter was contagious. Just walk down the street and smile at someone; they'd almost always smile back. And the ones who didn't smile were dried-up inside, as if they had raisins for hearts. They deserved happiness, everybody deserved happiness, but they hadn't learned to accept it, treasure it, soak it up like a sponge.

Hunkering down, Gabe opened the cabinet beneath the sink and retrieved two huge sponges, the kind you might use to scrub a car.

"You really do have sponges!" she exclaimed.

"Yup. Also car polish, furniture polish, a screwdriver, a hammer and nails, gift wrap from Christmas presents, an extension cord, extra toothpaste, a new roll of dental floss, an emergency can of underarm deodorant so I won't offend anybody with my *manly* sweat, and an outdated calendar."

"Is the calendar provocative?"

"Not unless you consider the Cheyenne Mountain Zoo provocative. I'm addicted to wild animals. Lions and tigers and—"

"Bars, oh my."

"Bars?"

"Bears. Long story." She hesitated, her face solemn. "Knickers's father was supposedly 'et by a bar.' "

"No, honey. He wasn't et by a bear. Don't you remember? He simply traveled around a lot."

"Poor Lady Scarlet. I'd hate to be in love with a man who left me at the drop of a hat. Especially if he 'borrowed' all my money."

"I promise I'll never borrow your money, Hallie, and I haven't encountered any bears lately, except for the teddy bear inside my studio. But I have bars. Of soap. This cabinet's a catchall."

"Most people use their kitchen drawer for a catchall."

"My kitchen's a kitchenette. When we build our dream house I'll give you drawers large enough to hold our firstborn."

"William Shakespeare Quinn," she murmured, wondering if Knickers had borne babies.

Rising to his feet, Gabe towered above her. "What did you say? I didn't hear you."

"I said teach me how to play sponge, Mr. Quinn."

"The rules aren't very difficult, Ms. O'Brien." Dropping both of the porous products into the sink, he rotated the hot and cold water faucets. Then he reached for Hallie's shirttails.

She stared into his gray-green eyes while he unbuttoned her shirt and unsnapped her bra. His desire for her was plainly visible, but she wondered if his eyes had expressed the same desire for Jennifer Bernadette et cetera.

"I love you, Hallie," he said, answering her thought. "Only you. This is the first time for both of us."

"The fifth time," she corrected.

"Don't be so pragmatic."

"But I *am* pragmatic, Gabe. That's why my visions and obsolete speak are so unusual, so jolting."

"Hush. Forget visions. Forget Gabriel and Knickers. My bathroom can only accommodate two sponge game players. Are you ticklish?"

"I don't know."

"Didn't your brother ever tickle you?"

"Neil was a play-the-stereo-so-loud-she-won't-bother-me kind of brother. Then I started to grow breasts and he was too embarrassed."

"What about other guys? Ivan, for instance?"

"How'd you know about Ivan?"

"Josh. You told Josh you were 'practically engaged.' "

"Honestly, Gabe, I'm not practically anything. Ivan talked about marriage, a stock market merger of sorts. The dividends would be kids, one boy and one girl, no more, no less. Eventually, if I played a dutiful wife, entertaining clients . . ." She felt her cheeks flush. "If I played hostess at his dinner parties and attended various social events, our stock would rise accordingly. Ivan's much more pragmatic than I. He didn't think I was adorable. He treated me like an accessory, an expensive watch fob. I could still dabble in art, that's what he called it, dabbling, but he didn't want me to mingle with all those raunchy 'bohemians,' especially the ones who painted . . ." She lowered her voice. "Nudes."

"Ivan and Jenn were made for each other," Gabe muttered.

Hallie buried her gaze in her sneakers. "I didn't want Josh to get the wrong impression, my sudden visit and all, but I'm sorry I lied."

"Well, honey, 'practically engaged' has a ring of truth to it, especially the practical part."

"What were we talking about? Oh, yes, tickles. Maybe I was waiting for *your* tickles."

"A wise decision." Removing her shirt and bra, he folded them over a towel rack. Then he retrieved a sponge and cleansed her upper body.

She didn't feel ticklish. She felt throbbish.

"Your turn," Gabe said, handing her the other sponge.

He was ticklish. Laughing with unrestrained joy, he helped her tug his shirt up over his head. Since laughter was contagious, she joined in while she carefully washed away the rivulets of perspiration that stained his back and chest. She noted that the muscles that rippled beneath her touch were more defined than her Archangel's. His drawn breath loosened the waistband of his shorts. Glancing down, she sneak-previewed his salute.

"Feet," he said, his voice somewhat hoarse. "Sit."

"Where?"

"The commode, the tub's rim, the floor, you choose."

Her legs felt languorous so she chose the floor, and immediately saturated the seat of her shorts. On his knees, Gabe took off her right sneaker and sock. The second sneaker developed a knotted lace. Undaunted, he yanked it free from her heel, then stripped away her second sock. Meanwhile, his sponge had been soaking nicely in the sink.

He cleansed her soles, then her toes, one by one, and Hallie couldn't believe the galvanic excitement she experienced, as if her feet were wired to the core of her sensations.

"Let me do your feet," she pleaded, "so that we can get on with our game."

For the first time, Gabe lost his composure. "I think we should skip my feet," he said. "A woman's dirty toes smell little girlish, tomboyish, while a man's dirty toes smell—"

"Are you planning to make love wearing sneakers?"

"No." Rising, he shed his sneakers and socks, then held each foot beneath the sink faucets.

He looks totally graceful, thought Hallie, knowing that if she tried the same trick she'd be hopping around like an off-balance, one-legged kangaroo. It had something to do with height. It had everything to do with height. Six-foot-plus people didn't worry about bending their knees over a sink. In her next life she wanted to be six-foot-plus. Imagine how easy it would be to shave her legs.

She wanted to share her bon mot with Gabe, but the "next life" bit stopped her cold. He might believe she had invited Knickers and Gabriel into the bathroom again.

And yet, it didn't really matter which room she occupied. Until she solved the Gabriel-Knickers mystery, she'd be haunted by the voice of Knickers, haunted by her Cripple Creek paintings.

"I'll meet you later, Mary Knickers," she blurted. "Inside the costume alcove."

"Hallie!" Gabe nearly fell over backwards.

"I'm not trancing, Gabe, honest. I just . . ." Her breath caught in her throat as she watched him draw his shorts down his long legs. The shorts had a built-in jockstrap so she could now study his salute in all its naked glory.

Mesmerized, she felt him wrap her fingers around a sponge.

She was sitting with her legs stretched out in front of her. Gabe settled his knees alongside her thighs. His eyes were slits of pleasure as she commenced to wash between his legs.

"My turn," he said, "or there won't be any turns left. Our game will be over. In any case, I want to prolong the agony."

"Agony?"

"Exquisite agony."

She understood what he meant by exquisite agony when he took off her shorts and undies, then sponged between her legs: a unique sensation.

The floor was very wet now, and so was she. Tossing the sponge away, Gabe managed to retrieve a towel from the towel rack, lower her upper body to the floor, fold the towel, then place it underneath her head. On his knees, hovering above her, holding her wrists motionless with his hands, his lips began to explore.

She arched toward his salute. She felt a primitive desire to scratch his back, but her wrists were still pinioned. A shivery sizzle consumed her and she truly believed she might short-circuit. Before that could happen, Gabe sheathed himself in the saturated warmth he had created.

By the time he released her wrists, a sensual deluge had engulfed her and she was unable to flex her fingers, much less scratch. Instead, she accepted his driving thrusts passively, letting the coil of electricity inside her body build, flow, ignite, until she quivered mindlessly, embracing the bursts of pleasure as her due, knowing his pleasure duplicated hers. That knowledge released her temporary immobility and she urged him on with her voice and body until, cresting, they both achieved a climax at the same time.

Afterwards, incapable of movement again, she said, "That was some gullywhomper."

"Gullywhomper?"

"Torrent. Outpouring." She felt a blush stain her cheekbones. "Overflow."

"Honey, if we live to be a hundred, and I hope we do, I'll never get enough of your obsolete-speak."

"If we live to be a hundred, and I hope we do," she said, "I'll never get enough of our gullywhompers."

An hour later, clean on the outside, satiated with love, laughter and lunch on the inside, she clutched a paintbrush in her right hand.

She never outlined her paintings. Sometimes she worked from a variety of pencil sketches and sometimes she worked from photos, but even before her Cripple Creek renderings, all her paintings had evolved from the images inside her head. She likened it to an author who didn't write a chapter-by-chapter outline.

In fact, a friend who wrote a successful mystery series had once confessed that she stared at her blank computer screen then filled it in with type.

"I know what you mean," Hallie had said. "I stare at my blank canvas then cover it with paint."

Now she stared at her blank canvas. Her knuckles were taut and her heart fluttered wildly, as if she'd trapped a slew of hummingbirds inside her rib cage.

Hand suspended, she shut her eyes. When she looked again, nothing had changed. The canvas was pristine, spotless, *virginal,* she thought without humor. Because she couldn't conjure up one image of Cripple Creek or Knickers.

Her paradoxical muse was on vacation.

Chapter Twenty-Four

Gabe studied the dancers, frozen in motion.

They weren't fleshed out yet, but they looked as if they might soon become the chorus line for a new ballet.

Duck Lake?

Swan Mountain?

Directly behind the dancers, Hallie had painted the Broadmoor Hotel's duck pond, complete with ducks. In the distance, majestic mountains escalated, their snowy peaks cresting at the top of the canvas: waves rather than ridges. She had effected a fiery sunset, a superlative blend of synchronic colors, all the more startling since the pond, ducks, mountains and dancers were lackluster, badly in need of mystic shadows and vivid hues.

"It's not finished," she understated.

Art is for the birds, thought Gabe, scrutinizing one of the swan ballerinas then shifting his gaze to the ducks. But he didn't dare say his pun out loud, especially since Hallie's beautiful eyes brimmed over with tears.

"I don't get it." Lightly, he ran his thumbs beneath her lower lashes, capturing the salty beads. "You were almost inconsolable after painting Cripple Creek. Now you're upset because you're normal again."

"I'm not normal."

Stepping back, away from Gabe's thumbs, Hallie almost bumped into a rack of costumes. The alcove's racy lingerie mocked her as she tugged at her T-shirt, decorated with the smiling face of Little Stevie Wonder. The shirt was too tight, inching above her belly button. Why had she worn it? Why had she packed it? The tee had belonged to her mom and it was in mint condition, considering that it had survived the sixties, seventies, eighties and nineties—just like Stevie Wonder.

"I'm not normal," she repeated. "I'm a picture puzzle that's missing a whole bunch of pieces. I'm incomplete."

"Two short hours ago we indulged in a mutual sponge bath that left us both fulfilled. Why do you feel incomplete?"

"Don't equate sex with creativity, Gabe."

"Sex *is* creativity."

"Okay. You're right. Of course you're right."

"Then why the tears?"

Facing the costume rack, she fingered a hula skirt. "I wanted to solve my Cripple Creek mystery," she said, "but I can't do that without painting Knickers and Gabriel."

"The mystery's solved, little love. Knickers and Gabriel lived happily ever after, to quote my brother's fairy tale author." Disentangling Hallie's fingers from the Polynesian dance costume, Gabe clasped her hands in his. "Honey, listen to me. I think you began trancing at an early age, making up imaginary playmates. You were lonely, unhap—"

"Horsefeathers! I didn't need imaginary playmates. My childhood was very happy. I might have been a tad shy, but I attended the requisite number of slumber parties. I belonged to the high school art squad and I was on the staff of the school magazine as art editor, and I dated, mostly double-dated. I wasn't terribly popular because I wouldn't go all the way . . ." She paused, her cheeks crimson. "My mom and dad were the best parents a girl could hope for. They didn't spoil me or smother me. They loved me. My brother rarely teased, at least not in a nasty way." She withdrew her hands from Gabe's and spread her arms. "My imagination soared—"

"That's what I'm talking about. Your imag—"

"Wait. Let me finish. My brother Neil followed his dream while I followed mine. An art scholarship. Paris. Success in my chosen field. I was brought up in a house filled with music. I wasn't sad or lonely, Gabe, quite the opposite."

When he merely stared down at her, she said, "Maybe I painted Gabriel because I was unfulfilled, sexually unfulfilled, but my Cripple Creek scenes . . ." She shook her curls. "I think there's a lesson to be learned, but I can't figure out what the lesson *is*. I only know that my paintings were the start of a quest."

"Hallie, your lesson was love and your so-called quest was me. I'm sorry if that sounds egotistical. Usually I prefer logic, like you, and yet I truly believe that something or somebody brought us together. Call it fate or kismet or astral influences or—"

"Death and destruction."

"What?"

"Death and destruction," she repeated, tugging at her shirt again, then thrusting her hands inside the pockets of her faded jeans. "Why did I get the blue devils when my mom mentioned Myers Avenue? Why did I feel a sorrowful ache when I stood at the intersection of Myers and Third?"

"The fire."

"I don't think so."

"Okay. How about Scarlet's funeral?"

"I'm Knickers, not Scarlet."

"Wouldn't Knickers have felt a sorrowful ache at the loss of her beloved Mama Scarlet?"

"Of course. But Knickers was fifteen or sixteen while I'm twenty-eight."

"Twenty-seven."

"I'll be twenty-eight May eighteenth, close enough."

"Are you saying that your 'sorrowful aches' were grown-up pangs?"

She nodded. "I think my aches, or pangs if you prefer, have something to do with a runaway horse, hitched to a buckboard. That's what I pictured in New York, just before I started painting Cripple Creek. One other thing, Gabe. I didn't mention it at the time because we had just kissed outside your friend Joe's casino and I wanted to sustain . . . prolong the exquisite agony. But I . . . well, to be perfectly honest, I lost my breath."

"So did I."

"You did?"

"I lose my breath every time we kiss."

"Dammit, Gabe, I'm serious. I didn't lose my breath from kissing. I lost my breath from . . . from paranormal influences."

Gabe stifled his instinctive flinch by glancing around the costume alcove. The room was fairly large, well-ventilated, but today it felt oppressive and smelled of paint. How could she work in here without becoming dispirited?

"I think we need a change of scenery," he said. "Follow me."

Hallie bird-dogged Gabe's white T-shirt and jean-clad butt outside the house.

Together, they climbed a rustic staircase to the redwood deck. She shut her eyes then opened them again, all but blinded by the panoramic view.

Forget God's feet and knees, she thought irreverently. *These mountains tickle God's belly.*

Gabe had been right about privacy. Behind the house was a wooded area. Evergreen trees spread their branches in gestures of supplication. Multicolored oak leaves formed patchwork parasols, protecting the pointy headed pines.

Protecting them from what? Snow? Torrential rainstorms? Evil spirits?

Twilight had begun to descend. The sky looked like an enormous palette, paint-streaked with pink and lilac and gold.

Terror stabbed through her. She shuddered, then silently chastised herself.

It's just a sunset, you silly goose. It can't hurt you. Gabe will protect you from things that go bump in the sky.

"But who will protect him?" she whispered.

"What did you say, honey?"

"The sky looks like a backdrop for a theatrical production, a brand-new musical called *Somewhere Over the Rainbow*, starring Gabriel Q and Alice W. O'Brien. Unfortunately, Alice can't carry a tune, even if she does carry a ghost."

"If my mountains can't convince you to stay," he said, ignoring her ghost reference, "nothing will."

"Colorado's beautiful," she acknowledged. "But I'll make my decision tomorrow night, after we visit Cripple Creek."

"Your decision shouldn't have anything to do with Cripple Creek. Why obsess over the past when we have our whole future ahead of us?"

"I'm not obsessing."

"Yes, you are."

Removing her hands from her pockets, grasping the deck's wooden rail, she gazed toward a distant peak. "If I'm haunted—"

"Bedeviled!"

"—by Cripple Creek, it's because we're connected, you and I. Is it merely a coincidence that Knickers loved an artist named Gabriel? Is it a coincidence that he lost his leg?"

"I didn't lose my leg. I injured my knee. And just for the record, my face isn't scarred." Ruefully, Gabe ran his finger across the small brand that marred his chin. "When you were sick, you said Gabriel scarred his face during a mine explosion. His face could shatter glass, you said. Remember?"

"Yes." Silent, she pondered for a few moments. Finally, she said, "You're badly scarred on the inside. Gabriel's snooty fiancée couldn't deal with his accident, just like Jenn."

"That's so far-fetched, it doesn't even deserve a comment, but I'll make one. Jenn and I weren't destined to spend our lives together. We've always been mules, hitched to a buckboard, stubborn mules, both pulling in opposite directions. No. That's not true. I was hitched to the buckboard. Jenn prefers a shiny carriage embossed with twenty-four-carat gold."

"How do you know I don't prefer a shiny carriage?"

"Do you?"

"To be perfectly honest, yes." She pictured Amelia Capshaw, her seat companion during her flight from New York. "I prefer first-class to coach, good wine to so-so wine, and I *hate* buckboards."

"How many buckboards have you encountered lately?"

"Don't change the subject!"

He looked perplexed. "I thought Jenn and buckboards *were* the subject."

"No, Gabe. The subject is similarities."

"What similarities? You had a happy childhood. Knickers didn't."

"Why do you say that? Because she was brought up in a parlor house?"

"Whorehouse."

"You say tomato, I say tomahto. Anyway, I was talking about grown-up similarities. The Gabriel connection."

"Sounds like a movie," Gabe said, striving for humor. "*The Gabriel Connection*, starring Mel Gibson."

She didn't crack a smile. "How do you explain my paintings and dreams?"

"You've probably been dreaming all along, and the paintings were inspired by your nocturnal visions."

"Nocturnal? Bilgewater! Up until last summer, I counted maybe three sheep before conking out completely. Even my catnaps were deep and dreamless."

Turning away from the rail, she stared up into his eyes. "Assuming you're right, Gabe, why did I envision Cripple Creek in the first place?"

"Most people have paranormal dreams of one kind or another. Following my knee surgery, I was confined to a hospital bed. My roommate was addicted to TV talk shows. Our TV was suspended from the ceiling like a bloated spider. I tried to catch up on my reading, but spiders are mesmerizing. One late-afternoon guest—on *Oprah*, I believe—was a noted psychiatrist who talked about dreaming across space and time. He even gave examples."

"Such as?"

"Let me think. There was a young, unmarried, professional woman in her late twenties."

"What a coincidence!"

"She dreamed she had entered a singing contest where the first prize was five hundred dollars. But Sandra, that was her name, couldn't decide what to sing. Jazz? Alternative rock? Country-western? Desperate, she chose an old gospel song. In her dream, she belted out the song. At the same time she saw a little Vietnamese boy, about six years old. 'Do they really give people five hundred dollars for singing?' he asked."

"Gabe, I don't understand how—"

"Now we get to the gist of the dream. The night before, Sandra's father had phoned her from Chicago. He'd seen an ad for a job in South Bend, Indiana, that he thought might interest her. Her parents lived in Chicago, only a couple of hours away from South Bend, and Sandra took that as a veiled hint that she move closer to home. She lived in Boston and loved it there, so she was faced with a situation in which her father tried to influence her without really understanding her point of view. The singing contest took her back to her childhood and reminded her of the many times she had to perform in areas that met the needs of her parents. Singing was her mother's thing. Mommy dearest even insisted that Sandra join the school glee club and church choir. The five hundred dollars had several meanings. It was the amount of money she'd once borrowed from her father and never repaid, so she felt indebted. It also brought to mind the Indianapolis 500, conjuring up images of dangerous competition and the excitement of winning. Competition and excelling were very important values in her home."

"What about the little boy?"

"He reminded Sandra of her own naïve acceptance of her parents' lifestyle. Being Vietnamese and a boy emphasized the fact that Sandra thought of herself as different."

"Interesting, Gabe, but what does that have to do with Knickers and Gabriel?"

"Nothing. It has to do with you. Haven't you been stressed lately? I don't mean us. I'm talking in general."

"I suppose I have been stressed. My gallery opening and . . . everything."

Grasping the rail again, Hallie tried to remember what had occurred just before she'd begun painting Gabriel and Cripple Creek. First, she had moved into her own apartment, a monumental decision. Her father had objected with the usual it-isn't-safe-for-a-single-girl admonishment.

Second, her brother had championed a lasting relationship with Ivan, insisting that marriage would bring status, respectability and kids. Hadn't Neil even mentioned her biological clock?

Third, Ivan had initiated an aggressive seduction, not quite a rape. She had managed to wriggle free from his tentacles by slapping his face. Hard. Twice. Furious, he had called her a tease and accused her of being frigid. The next day he apologized. Profusely. She accepted his apology, but, in her own mind, his not-quite-a-rape had soured the relationship.

Had she been jealous over Marianne's pregnancy?

No. Yes. Despite her craving for independence, she wanted kids. Kids required a husband, at least it did for her. She didn't love Ivan—had even begun to fear him—so that had led to her portrait of Gabriel.

What about the parlor house paintings? Was there a sexual connotation?

"Gabe, did the psychiatrist mention sex?"

"Of course. What's an afternoon talk show without sex? Ratings would be nil. The psychiatrist said that sometimes sexual imagery expressed feelings of closeness and intimacy. However, sometimes it's a defense to ward off those feelings. Control or loss of control may be expressed in sexual images."

"But I was in control," she whispered. "Wasn't I?"

"A person who has been excessively inhibited might express his or her sexuality in dreams," Gabe stated, pulling the words from his memory.

Moving directly behind her, he circled her waist with his hands. "You're not inhibited, little love," he teased, "quite the opposite."

She leaned back against the broad expanse of his chest, enjoying his solid strength. "Are you saying that I invented Knickers because I was exposed to sexual stimulation without consummation? Or that, feeling stressed, I traveled across time and space, encountering Scarlet? The same way Sandra encountered the little Vietnamese boy?"

"I'm not saying anything. I'm merely paraphrasing a TV psychiatrist." He nuzzled her nape. "I don't have any answers, honey. Wish I did. Then we could put all this behind us and get on with our lives."

"I'll try painting my primed canvas," she stated, her voice decisive. "The one that depicted the fire. Maybe I can conjure up Knickers. Or Gabriel. Or both. What time do we leave for Cripple Creek?"

"Noon, if you want to explore first."

"That gives me tonight and tomorrow morning to try and paint something other than ducks and dancers." Making an about-face, she gazed up into his eyes. "Please don't be mad."

"I'm not mad, Hallie. I just wish you'd accept happily ever after."

She wanted to give in to his words, his caresses, the serenity of the landscape, and yet she couldn't stop her mind from posing two questions.

Were her trances and paintings the result of unmet sexual tensions?

Did Knickers and Gabriel disappear because Gabe dissolved all inhibitions?

Leaning back against Gabe again, she felt him cross her heart with his fingers.

Maybe I should book an appearance on Oprah, she thought. *The ratings would soar. Just like I soar every time Gabe touches my heart.*

Hallie chewed the end of her paintbrush.

Her canvas depicted . . . ballerinas.

This time, rather than *Swan Lake*, she had painted *Giselle*.

The dominant male dancer looked like Mikhail Baryshnikov, who had made his American Ballet Theatre debut—his U.S. debut—in *Giselle.* Hallie had seen his performance from inside her mom's belly, another family joke. Neil liked to say that she painted ballerinas because of that prenatal experience.

"I give up," she told Mikhail.

Maybe I'll try again tomorrow, she thought, joining Gabe in front of the TV. They watched a movie. After it was over, she couldn't remember if it had been about aliens or alienation.

In bed, Gabe seemed to understand that she wanted cuddling, not sex.

Dovetailed against his body, she felt comforted by the perfect fit, as if they were two pieces of a broken vase welded together without any perceptible fissure.

She fell into a fitful slumber and dreamed she was on top of a mountain, somewhere over the rainbow.

Was the landscape Oz or Ozone? She saw lions and tigers and bears, oh my, but she couldn't see one happy little bluebird. Instead, raucous crows perched on the bristled pine trees and stately oaks below.

"Go 'way," she murmured in her sleep. "I'm over the rainbow. I want to see happy little bluebirds fly."

In a flash, the glossy-feathered crows vanished, swallowed up by a darkness that descended without warning. Just as suddenly, a comet appeared, its fuzzy head and long tail phosphorescent.

The comet didn't streak across the sky. It stayed overhead, suspended by invisible wires. Its luminescent tail seemed to wag like a dog. Or a very skinny, very hostile crocodile.

She wanted to run away, but her bare feet danced a Michael Jackson moonwalk.

Illuminated by the comet, several lions and tigers and bears surged forward.

To her surprise, they were all enormous stuffed animals, the kind you might win at a carnival. Their pacesetter was Gabe's prop teddy bear.

As she stood motionless, the animals surrounded her, their plush bodies pressing closer and closer until she couldn't breathe.

The teddy bear hugged her. "I love you, Knickers," he said.

"I love you, Gabriel." Hallie whispered the words in the darkness of the bedroom.

"Don't leave me!"

Half asleep, half awake, she couldn't determine if the plea had been Gabe's or Gabriel's.

"I'll never leave you," she cried, turning her head and punctuating her words with soft kisses against the hollow of Gabe's throat.

His arms tightened around her. But even in the warmth of his embrace, there was no escape. She could sense the crows gloating. Behind her closed eyelids, she could see the pulsating nucleus of a comet. Only this time it wasn't suspended. This time it streaked across the sky.

Her dream faded into nothingness, a whim-wham of vague superficiality. No longer over the rainbow, she had, somehow, clicked her heels three times and wished herself home.

Home. Gabe meant home. She burrowed closer to him, her face sharing his pillow, her body craving something she couldn't even identify.

Possession?

No. Protection.

Chapter Twenty-Five

"Dammit, magpie," Hallie said, "if 'death and destruction' is the answer to my quest, I can deal with it."

Her black-and-white plumaged companion merely beaked seed from the feeder outside the costume alcove's open window. And despite Hallie's fervent declaration, her canvas remained blank.

Early—very early—this morning she had painted a new dance sequence. Dominating her canvas, a Shirley Jones clone looked as if she knew that love was all around while a Toulouse-Lautrec Moulin Rouge dancer (who bore a striking resemblance to Robert Preston) seemed to be singing: "We've got trouble, right here in Colorado, and that starts with C, and that rhymes with D, and that stands for *dream*."

In another time, another place, Hallie's impression of her Impressionistic painting might have been funny. Or, at the very least, ironic. But right now, this very minute, it was time for some serious O'Brien logic—unchurned by emotion.

First, she had created the six original Cripple Creek paintings because she couldn't deliberately bring those events to mind. Same for the bullfight, the fire, and the funeral procession.

Second, her fevered musings had probed her subconscious, so now she couldn't paint Knickers.

"Does that make any sense, magpie?"

Only a few short weeks ago she had quoted Vincent van Gogh: *I dream my paintings and then I paint my dreams.*

Unfortunately, Vinnie's philosophy didn't hold true for Alice W. O'Brien.

When her dreams were subconscious, she painted. If she remembered her dreams, she couldn't paint, at least she couldn't paint Knickers and Cripple Creek.

Dancers were a different story.

"Dammit, Maggie! I want to paint the Gabriel-Knickers story. Or is it more honorable to leave them alone? If I dabble in their lives, will I change the course of history?"

Her newly christened magpie continued to beak seed. It looked like one of those bobbing toys seen from the back window of an old car.

"Featherbrained mooncalf!" Hallie chastised herself, not the bird. "What makes you think you're changing history? You're reliving history. What's so honorable about that?

Honor—an old-fashioned word. Honor described one whose worth brought respect. For example, a person could be an *honor* to his or her profession. She had never thought about herself in those terms. The paint she spread across her canvas was akin to the lifeblood that flowed through her veins, a vital force. If she achieved fame, as well as respect, so much the better.

Gabe had taken the world by storm, his expressive, sometimes merciless photos establishing his honorable reputation.

What about Knickers and Gabriel? Knickers had a reputation. Due to circumstances beyond her control, it wasn't exactly an honorable one. Gabriel, however, was a well-respected artist. Collectors had clamored for his canvases. But Hallie, schooled in art history, had never heard of him. She knew, from her fevered dreams, that he'd signed his paintings "Gabriel"—no last name—but artists often used only one name. Cher. Madonna. Modigliani. Had Gabriel dropped out of sight, suddenly, before his reputation could become firmly established?

Last Tuesday night she had avidly read Cripple Creek's promotional pamphlets. They had mentioned such experts—their word—as Pearl DeVere, Nell McClusky, and Lola Livingston, parlor house denizens. But the pamphlets hadn't mentioned a "Mary Knickers" or "Lady Scarlet." Hallie had been disappointed but not surprised. After all, her mother's carefully compiled computer records and history books didn't include the Homestretch.

Legal documents would have burned in the Cripple Creek fire.

Even if documents or chronicles did exist, Hallie couldn't investigate. She didn't know any last names. Scarlet . . . Mary . . . Gabriel . . . needles in a haystack.

She pictured a haystack, situated next to a scarecrow.

Scarecrow. Gabe's dopey nickname. Gabe wanted her to forget the past.

He was probably right, so she'd simply concoct her own story ending. The Gabriel-Knickers story, starring Mel Gibson and . . . Julia Roberts? No. Her hair was too auburn. Nicole Kidman? No. Her hair was too light. Hallie tried to envision an actress with hair the color of ripe strawberries.

"Are you still listening, Maggie? Gabriel and Knickers travel to Paris, have ten children, and live happily ever after. Their paintings hang in the Louvre."

The bird flew skyward, just as Hallie heard the imperative ring of a telephone. With a sense of guilt, she realized she hadn't called Marianne or her parents. Funny. In New York, living only a few miles away, she called them almost every day. Well, she'd been sick, hadn't she? And busy.

Busy exploring Cripple Creek.

Busy trancing.

Busy surviving the flu.

Busy playing tennis.

Busy painting dancers.

Busy making love, she thought with a vivid blush.

Hi, Mom and Dad. Sorry I haven't called, but I've been loving Mr. Gabe Quinn a lot lately. Marianne told me about this O-word, introduced by "Sesame Street" 's Elmo. So, naturally, I had to discover its meaning for myself.

Hallie focused on her blank canvas, primed white after her doltish *Music Man* distraction. If she retrieved her Polaroid snapshot, the one with the comet, and copied it line for line, color for color, maybe then her paradoxical muse would—

"Forget the past," said Gabe, entering the alcove. "We now have a future."

"What do you mean 'we,' Drac?"

He strode forward and nuzzled her neck. "I vant to devour every portion of your body," he huffed into her ear. "But I'm too excited."

"How can excitement prevent you from devouring my body? And what did you mean by your cryptic 'future' remark?"

"It's not cryptic. It's great. Fantastic."

"Gabe!"

"Okay, okay." He stepped back and gave her a boy-with-his-hand-caught-in-the-cookie-jar grin. "The White House just called."

"The White House White House?"

"No, the purple White House."

"But it's Sunday."

"The government doesn't work on Sunday?"

"Not unless there's an emergency. Or it's something important. Something important just happened, right?"

"Yup. The president made an *important* request." This time Gabe's smile looked smug. "He wants *me,* Hallie, for his personal photographer. A staff member called and asked if I could catch the red-eye flight, share breakfast with the prez tomorrow. I said Tuesday would be more convenient."

"Convenient," she echoed.

" 'Tuesday will be fine, Mr. Quinn,' the staff member said, smooth as silk, and . . . why aren't you dancing for joy?"

"I might knock over my painting."

"What painting? It's a blank canvas. Let's dance together. We can borrow two hula skirts from the rack and—"

"No, Gabe."

"Hallie, what's wrong? I thought you'd be happy for me."

"I *am* happy."

"If that's happy, they'll have to rewrite the dictionary."

"Maybe I'm not dancing because I feel as though I'm losing you."

"To whom? The president?"

"Yes. No. Yes. Won't he send you on various assignments?"

"Of course."

"Overseas?"

"Sure. But I'll come back. And I'll be careful, very careful, now that *you're* waiting for me."

"Waiting. Yes. That's a good idea."

"What's a good idea?"

"You fly to Washington while I fly home. After my gallery show, we can meet someplace."

"That's a stupid idea. I want you in Washington, D.C. It'll be my home base. We can find an apartment, a house, whichever you prefer, and you can decorate it with unique antiques. We can even build our dream house, the one with the huge kitchen drawers and sloped bath—"

"No."

"No?" He quirked an eyebrow. "Why not?"

"I'd be living all alone in a strange city."

"I'll introduce you to the president's wife."

"Don't joke, Gabe."

"What else can I do? Beg?"

"Of course not. You can cultivate patience. And wait."

"Until?"

"Until you've established the limits of your job."

"There *are* no limits. That's what makes it so exciting."

"Not to me. I don't think I could deal with an absentee hus . . . lov . . . friend. I can't even deal with absentee ghosts."

"Aha! Now I understand why you're so hesitant. You think Gabriel walked out on Knickers and you don't want history repeating itself."

No. I was thinking about Lady Scarlet, who lived on crumbs. And hope.

Aloud she said, "I hadn't considered that, Gabe, but you could be right. When we last left Gabriel, he was starting to get rich. And famous. Maybe you'll get caught up in politics and—"

"Don't you trust me, Hallie?"

"Yes."

"Don't you love me?"

"Yes."

"Don't you trust my love for you?"

"Yes." She took a deep breath. "Why are you so stubborn? What difference does it make if we wait a few months?"

"None."

His voice sounded curt, too curt. "Our love," she said, "will survive."

"I suppose it will."

She wanted to canoodle against him, hug him, kiss him, but she didn't know how to pierce the invisible suit of armor he had just slipped into. Even his face looked inscrutable, veiled by an invisible helmet and visor.

"It's almost noon," she said. "Do you want to leave for Cripple Creek?"

"We can attend the melodrama at the Imperial Hotel, Hallie. The curtain rises at four-thirty and we already have our tickets. But right now I need to make some phone calls, canceling next week's photo sessions. I'm sorry."

"That's okay. I'll take a cloud bubble bath . . ." She paused, hoping he'd suggest they bathe together.

Instead, he turned on his heel and walked briskly through the open doorway.

He didn't slam the door, but she heard the sound of a slam just the same.

"Congratulations," she called, much too late and much too low.

Chapter Twenty-Six

"Hiss!"

"Boo!"

"Yay!"

"Ahhhh . . ."

Hallie halfheartedly shouted along with the rest of the audience. Why couldn't she get into the spirit of the melodrama?

Because her spirits were too low, that's why.

Gabe looked as if he'd been painted with ice: a thick coat of cadmium white, tinged with royal blue.

What was his problem?

She tried to concentrate on the players strutting across the stage, but her mind kept wandering.

What had she done wrong?

"Boo!"

"Yay!"

Yay for Alice W. O'Brien! She had finally broken free from her time warp by offering Gabe unrestricted freedom. He'd be totally involved with his new job, and he wouldn't have to worry about a wife . . . lover . . . friend.

Obviously, he didn't appreciate her self-sacrifice.

He was nothing more than a bullyragged jellyfish!

She had offered him elbow room and he'd mistakenly assumed *Brush-off*. With a capital B, and that rhymes with C, and that stands for . . . cold shoulder.

Perhaps he even equated her with Jenn.

How unfair!

Sadly, she waved good-bye to William Shakespeare Quinn, her firstborn. Because she knew that this morning's rift could never be resolved. Gabe wouldn't even discuss it. He'd spent the afternoon tracking down his clients. Most were at the Denver Broncos game, squelching the perception that women weren't interested in football, thank you very much, Andy Rooney.

Then Gabe had showered (alone) and joined her in the family room. Where, in an alien voice, each word coated with ice, he had apologized for the delay and complimented her on her outfit.

"You look like a spring garden," he had said, referring to her smock dress, appliquéd with colorful flowers. It was a dress she often wore to her gallery openings since it required a pair of high-heeled boots and made her look older.

Well . . . taller.

During the drive to Cripple Creek, Gabe had kept the discussion inconsequential.

And he kept apologizing for ruining her afternoon, her *last* afternoon.

No more appeals to stay. No more pleas to join him in Washington.

"Boo!"

"Hiss!"

"Boo!"

Tomorrow she'd call Josh, say good-bye, and casually discuss the reason for his brother's chilly attitude. She would ask Josh what the hell she'd done wron—

"Earth to Hallie."

"Huh?"

"It's intermission," said Gabe. "Would you like a glass of wine?"

"Dare I test the attitude? I mean, altitude?"

If he noticed her slip of the tongue, he ignored it. "I think you're safely insulated," he said. "After all, you've been here a week. That's plenty of time to adjust."

While they both sipped white wine, he talked about the melodrama, ironically called *In Old New York*.

How could he remember so many details? He'd been preoccupied, too.

"Are you having fun?" he asked.

"Absolutely," she fibbed. "This is a fun way to spend my last night."

Did he wince? Or had she imagined it?

They returned to their seats. She endured another half-hour of boos and yeas while her emotions churned. First anger, then despair, then regret, then anger again. Why was Gabe so cold and polite? Why was he treating her this way?

I did nothing wrong!

The players took their bows, then presented an olio, where they performed in front of the drawn curtain. They were good, very good, but Hallie wanted to leave. Whether Gabe approved or not, she wanted to walk down Myers Avenue one more time. One *last* time.

She didn't even care if she tranced. Trancing was better than living with unanswered questions.

What if nothing happened?

Then she'd concede that Gabe was right, that Knickers and Gabriel had lived happily ever after, after all.

Unlike Alice W. O'Brien and Gabriel Q.

"Let's beat the crowd, Drac," she whispered into Gabe's ear.

"You vant to hit the crowd," he whispered back, and for the first time all evening he smiled.

"Beat them to the exit, you featherbrained mooncalf. After three months of painting in my bare feet and one week of wearing sneakers, these high-heeled boots feel wobbly. I'd like to get a head start, if that's okay with you."

"Sure. Good idea. We can invade the Imperial Hotel's buffet." Grasping her elbow, he led her down the aisle. "Or would you prefer another restaurant?"

"I'd prefer a stroll down Myers Avenue. Do you mind terribly?"

"Why would I mind?" He dropped her elbow.

"I don't know. You've been acting so distant, so different."

"I'm not acting, Hallie. The Imperial Players act. Jenn acts. You act. Watch your step," he cautioned, as they crossed the threshold and exited the hotel.

"Wait! Gabe, wait! Don't walk so fast."

He made an abrupt about-face. "I'm tired of waiting, Hallie. I want a home and a family and—"

"So do I! Dammit, Gabe, I wasn't acting out some role when I said I loved you."

"I think you were. I think you were playing Knickers to my Gabriel."

"That's ridiculous."

"Do you want me to wager for you, Hallie? I would, only I can't figure out who owns you."

"Nobody owns me!"

"New York owns you."

"What does *that* mean?"

"It means you can't sever the ties to your family."

"My family has nothing to do with this."

"What about your paranormal family? Knickers and Gabriel. You can't relinquish the past and you won't consider living in the present. Forget the future. You won't even take a chance on the future."

"Now just one doggone minute, Mr. Quinn. After your *important* phone call you raced into my studio—"

"My costume alcove."

"—and announced that you had just accepted a new job. It was a fait accompli. You didn't ask my opinion. You didn't tell the president—"

"The president's staff member."

"—that you'd talk it over with your lover."

"How could I say 'lover' during a professional conversation? Especially while conversing with the White House?"

"One doesn't converse with a house."

"One does if it's the White House." He took a deep breath. "We talked it over."

"No, Gabe, we didn't. You *assumed* I'd meekly follow you to Washington." He looked as if he might interrupt again, so she held up one hand, palm out. "You bribed me with antiques, like . . . like Josh bribes Napkin. But your antiques were nothing more than dog biscuits."

"Napkin doesn't go for bribes. He throws up on Chihuahuas. And why the hell are we discussing Napkin?"

"Okay, let's discuss Jenn."

"Let's not."

"Yesterday, before our tennis game, I told her that you said I reminded you of her. It was a joke, Gabe, but now I'm not so sure."

"I don't want to talk about Jenn."

"I think we should. I think it explains your altitude."

"Altitude?" He quirked an eyebrow.

"I meant attitude, and you know it!"

"Maybe you should have skipped that glass of wine during intermission. I think it's gone to your head."

"I think your head needs to be vacuumed. You're obsessed with hurtful memories."

"*I'm* obsessed? *You're* the one who wants to stroll down Myers Avenue."

They had come full circle, she thought, suddenly bone-tired. Gabe stood six, maybe seven feet away, but the chasm was too deep, uncrossable. How could she reach him?

Before she could reach him, physically, two men rounded the corner. They were drunk, almost reeling, and their scowly expressions suggested that they'd lost money, lots of money. The shorter, fatter man wore a sweat-stained cowboy hat, which he removed. Twisting its brim in his hands, he tried to whistle.

"Hey, sweet li'l lady," he said. "Where was you when I needed Lady Luck?"

"This sweet little lady is my little lady," Gabe stated. His voice sounded calm enough, but Hallie could see his shoulders stiffen.

"Aw, Bubba, leave 'er alone," the second man said. He looked like Icabod Crane, had Icabod Crane worn filthy overalls and an Oakland Raiders baseball cap.

"Shaddup, Roger," Bubba said. "You cost me a bundle this afternoon when your friggin' team lost to the friggin' Broncos. Then you pulled me 'way from the table 'fore I could win my money back."

"You didn't have no more money to bet."

"But you had enough for another beer, din'cha asshole?" Turning his face toward Hallie, Bubba lowered one hand, shaped it into a claw, and snaked it between his legs. "C'mon, sweetheart," he said, rocking on his heels, thrusting his pelvis forward. "Let's have ourselves some fun."

Enraged, Gabe swiftly crossed the invisible chasm. But it wasn't necessary.

Jabbing punches at Bubba's bloated face, Roger hollered, "Who you callin' asshole, asshole?"

Hallie had begun walking toward the curb and Gabe's car. She sensed Bubba's return punch, aimed at Roger, just before she felt it.

Staggering backwards, her wobbly heels caught a crack in the sidewalk.

The hotel's brick wall connected with her head.

She sank to the ground. It felt like slow-motion, but one didn't fall in slow-motion, especially when one got clunked by a wall.

Did one?

I think I'll play Napkin and throw up all over Bubba's cowboy boots.

That was her last coherent thought. As her stomach leapfrogged toward her throat, darkness closed over her.

She welcomed the black void with a glad cry.

Because she saw Gabriel.

All her senses kicked in. She could smell pipe tobacco. She could hear his low laughter. She could touch the corded muscles in his arms.

He was beautiful.

She had expected his face to be disfigured, like a movie monster, like *The Phantom of the Opera*'s phantom, like Beauty's Beast.

Instead, he had one small scar that cleaved his chin, one that slashed across the bridge of his nose, and one that separated his right eyebrow, arching it. The most prominent scar zigzagged from his left ear to his jaw, maybe a quarter of an inch in width. A modern-day plastic surgeon could probably reduce it to a hairline scar.

Why bother? The jagged line, pale in his tanned face, didn't detract from his dark eyes, full of joy. Or his thick black hair, tied at his nape with a piece of string. She was tempted to trace the scar with her finger. No. Her lips.

Why not do it? Gabriel stood in front of an easel, next to a tree, and his smile was far brighter, far warmer than the sun.

"I love you," he said. "You're everything I've ever wanted in a woman. Happiness can't describe the way I feel, although full to bursting comes mighty close."

A purr lapped at the back of her throat as Hallie swayed toward him. She reached up, planning to clutch his shoulders and press her body against the broad expanse of his chest, a chest that might have been etched from the granite that adorned Cripple Creek's Mount Pisgah.

Arms semicircled, fingers extended, she grasped empty air.

Then she saw Knickers.

Chapter Twenty-Seven

"I'm hungry," said the young woman. Her flawless skin was the color of café au lait, a smidgen more milk than coffee, and just like Lady Godiva, her long, cardinal-red hair hid the swell of her naked bosom.

"Okay, Knickers," said the man standing in front of an easel. "Let's share some bread, cheese and wine."

"I'd rather share kisses, Gabriel. Kisses are sweeter than wine."

He waved his arms and paint from two paintbrushes spattered the ground. "*Anybody's* kisses?"

"No, you featherbrained mooncalf. I'd rather taste *your* kisses."

"And how many other kisses have you tasted, little love?"

"None." She splayed her hands across her hips. "Are you saying that I should kiss another man and see if he measures up?"

"Would you do that?"

"Never! I'll taste your kisses till the day I die, Gabriel, and that's a sworn vow."

"Don't talk of dying, Knickers. You're only eighteen."

"Nineteen."

"What's today? May fifteenth?"

"May eighteenth, Gabriel. Nineteen hundred and ten," she added, although it wasn't necessary. He knew what year it was. Everybody did. The year of the comet. Halley's Comet.

"Damn me for a fool," he swore. "I clean forgot. Happy

birthday, Mary Knickers. Tonight we'll celebrate at a fancy restaurant, then stroll down Myers Avenue and watch the comet."

"I'd rather watch it from here, Gabriel."

"We've talked about this before, and you agreed."

"I didn't agree. I said I didn't want to quarrel."

"There might be a fireworks display," he bribed.

"I hate firecrackers. They hurt my ears."

"Such pretty ears." Dropping the brushes into a can of turpentine, he advanced behind her, nuzzled her neck, then licked one lobe.

"Bread, cheese, wine," she gasped.

"What about kisses?"

"After the wine." With a seductive smile, she shrugged her shoulders into the robe she wore in between poses. The robe was Gabriel's. Since she was tall, its bottom reached her ankles. She wound the sash around her waist twice and still had enough left for a bow.

What a heavenly day for a picnic, she thought. Last month the grassy fields had been shrouded with snow. In fact, she and Gabriel had been confined to their cabin by a raging blizzard. She had posed, he had painted, and they'd made love in front of the fireplace. She had rationed their food carefully, especially the flour and coffee, since they couldn't navigate the trail to Cripple Creek.

"We'll soon become ghosts," he had teased. "Skinny ghosts."

"Don't be silly, Gabriel. If Death comes knocking"—she'd fisted her small hands—"he'll be puking up teeth."

Today the aspen trees were shiny with flower catkins, signifying the end of winter. Knickers glanced up at the sun. She couldn't determine the time, but it had to be an hour past noon, maybe later. No wonder her tummy growled.

How could Gabriel forget the date? He had talked about the damnfool comet for weeks. No. Months. He wanted to paint it, Halley's Comet, streaking across the sky above Laura Bell's and Neil McClosky's and the Mikado and the Old Homestead. He said it was a "once in a lifetime opportunity."

Knickers felt her throat clog. Halley's Comet spelled out "yell shame" if you tangled the letters then dropped the C and T and one E.

Spreading a blanket across paint-spattered flowers, she shivered.

"Cold?" Somewhat awkwardly, Gabriel hunkered down and reached for a piece of cheese.

"No." She sat next to him, her appetite gone lickety-split away. "It's just that last night I dreamed about crows."

"I dreamed about your beautiful body."

"I'm serious, Gabriel. I saw at least a dozen crows, perched on the aspens. The crows were caw-cawing up a storm."

"There's no storm, little love, not even the hint of a cloud. Tonight the sky should be crystal-clear and the comet—"

"Mama Scarlet said that crows betokened danger. She dreamed about them the night before the fire."

"And how could you know that? You were only five years old."

"Mama Scarlet told me. She dreamed about crows and I dreamed about them, too. Crows and bears."

"Grizzly bears?"

"No. Toy bears. The stuffed ones, named for the president."

"But that's a good omen, Knickers. The teddy bear was named for Mr. Roosevelt because he refused to shoot a bear."

"My dream bears were big, Gabriel, bigger than you. They hugged me and I couldn't breathe."

"You can't breathe when I hug you."

"That's different, Gabriel. You take my breath away. The bears *stole* my breath."

Knickers crumbled a piece of cheese between her thumbs and fingers. Should she tell Gabriel about her other dream? The funny dream? Not ha-ha funny. Funny strange.

In her funny strange dream, she stood on top of the Gold Dollar Saloon's raised stage and watched Gabriel's poker game. He had just wagered his horse. An older girl watched, too. The older girl wore blue denim trousers, like the miners wore, and her hair was dark and curly, cropped short, above her shoulders.

Knickers interrupted her remembrance to make sure her own waist-length hair cascaded down her back. Gabriel liked to run his fingers through the sleek red strands, but tonight she'd pin it up. After all, she was a lady.

The girl inside the Gold Dollar Saloon had been a lady. Knickers didn't know how she knew that, but she did. Maybe it was because the girl looked so clean. And even in the dream she smelled like lemons. Whores usually smelled like muskrats, as if they hid their dirt beneath a layer of scent.

Mama Scarlet never smelled of musk. Until the day she died, Mama Scarlet bathed every day. Knickers had continued the tradition. Every morning Gabriel toted water from the well. He never complained, even though it was hard work. But he wouldn't let her tote the water. He said, "I want to wait on you hand and *foot*."

Now that they were wed, he could joke about his missing leg.

Smiling fondly, she watched him devour a hunk of bread, then wash it down with wine. He didn't hardly chew. She should chastise him for his lack of etiquette, but she didn't have the heart. He was thirty-three, and yet he looked like a mischievous boy.

Her smile faded when she thought about her one disappointment. She and Gabriel couldn't make babies. He said the fun was in the trying, but she didn't agree. The fun was in the having. She pictured her baby sister, Beatrice, so warm and cuddly, and without warning she had the blue devils.

With his finger, Gabriel tilted her chin. "What's wrong, honey?"

"The comet," she fibbed, even though it was only half a fib. "The comet scares me, Gabriel. Did you know that the miners won't work because they don't want to die underground? Quite a few went home to spend their last days with their families."

"Superstitious fools!" He released her chin. "They think the end of the world is at hand. You don't, do you?"

"Of course not." She watched an ant scurry toward a bread crumb. "After the blizzard, when we rode to town for supplies, Mr. Harper told me about this vender selling comet pills outside the Imperial Hotel. The pills are supposed to protect people from the comet's dire effects. We have lots of money banked, Gabriel. Could we buy some pills? Please?"

Leaning back against a tree, he pulled her unresisting body across his lap. "Knickers, listen and listen good. Edmund Halley himself observed the comet's passing in 1531 and 1607. It wasn't the end of the world then, and it won't be now."

"I saw a newspaper story inside Harper's Grocery. Mark Twain said he came in with Halley's Comet and expected to go out with it. And"—she took a deep breath—"he died last month!"

"What does that have to do with the price of beans?"

"Maybe he dreamed about crows."

Gabriel laughed. "I'm sorry, Knickers," he said, still chuckling. "I don't mean to make light of your fears, but you're not thinking straight. Mark Twain died because he was seventy-four years old. I saw another newspaper story yesterday, when I rode to town. It said people were hiding in cyclone cellars and caves. Do you want to burrow inside a cave, little love?"

"No! I'm not some bullyragged jellyfish. I'll watch your dangfool comet, Gabriel. I'll even paint it. Tomorrow. First thing. After my bath."

"That's my good girl. Eat your lunch."

"I'm not hungry anymore. Holy Moses! The sky's filled with clouds now, Gabriel, and it's thundering."

While she gathered the picnic items, he grabbed his painting and wooden crutch. She felt raindrops bead her long lashes. Maybe the rain would wash away her fears. Maybe the rain would wash away the comet.

She adjusted her long-legged stride to his choppy one as they headed toward the cabin.

Inside, it smelled like fresh-baked bread.

"What should I wear to your fancy restaurant, Gabriel?"

"Well, I don't know, Knickers. Your best gown's awfully short. And it's too tight across your bosom."

"My best and *only* gown's out of style, Gabriel. You could even say it's moss-grown."

"I should have bought you a pretty dress last Christmas, instead of that lacy bust enhancer. You don't need a bust enhancer, but you hinted and hinted . . ." He paused to heave a deep sigh. "Guess you'll have to wear a bedsheet."

"Bedsheet?"

"Yup. You're handy with a needle and thread. The one on the bed will do. It's washed and—"

"It is not! Last night we wrinkled the sheets something awful. See?" Casting aside a folding screen, nodding toward the bed, her gaze touched upon a box.

"Happy birthday, Knickers."

"Gabriel! You didn't forget."

"Open it."

"What a pretty box. It's from Johnson's Department Store."

"Open it."

"Men! Always so impatient." Slowly, she lifted the lid. "Oh, Gabriel, what a lovely gown."

"How can you tell? It's still inside the damnfool box."

"Don't call my pretty box foolish."

"Mary Knickers!"

"Hold your horses, Gabriel."

With a reverence reserved for Christmas, she drew the gown from the box, took off her damp robe, then held the blue and gold satin damask against her body.

"Elephant sleeves," she sighed. "I've always wanted elephant sleeves."

"Why didn't you say so? I would have trapped an elephant and cut off its sleeves."

"*Ears,* Gabriel. They're called elephant sleeves because they look like an elephant's ears. See how the material flares out before being gathered tightly at the waistband?"

"Nope."

"You don't?"

"All I can see is your naked body."

"Bilgewater. You look at my naked body every day. Who do you think poses for your paintings?"

"I've never seen your body hidden by elephant ears."

"*Sleeves,* Gabriel."

"Put the dress away."

"Why?" She saw the wicked light in his eyes. "Oh, no. We don't have time."

"Sure we do. We'll eat our fancy dinner after the comet."

"But I want to watch the comet through the restaurant's plate-glass window. It might be less . . ."

"Frightening?"

She nodded. "I'm playing jellyfish again, aren't I?"

"Yup." Carefully, he folded her beautiful new gown over the screen. Then he nuzzled her neck. "Your hair smells like rain," he said into her ear.

His huffy breath produced an instant wave of desire. So did his rough unshaven chin when he kissed the deep cleft between her breasts. She could hardly unbutton his trousers fast enough. "Now, Gabriel!" she cried, wild to have him.

"Soon, and that's a promise." Seated on the edge of the bed, he removed his boot and clothing. Then he stood, his balance remarkable for a man with only one leg. "I want to play elephant," he said. Clasping his fingers together, he swung his arms like an elephant's trunk, until his elbows bent and he captured her head between his arms. Then he kissed her.

She felt the familiar belly warmth, then the familiar weakness, and she sank back, onto the mattress.

Gabriel dropped to his good knee, spread her legs, and began his ministrations. His tongue was eager, her response immediate. She found his hands, placed them on her breasts, and arched her back. Flinging her arms over her head, she searched for something to hold onto. But there was nothing, so she buried her hands in the thickness of his hair, and when he finally molded his hard body to her pliant body, she welcomed his entry with a glad cry.

Afterwards, she twined her long legs about his waist,

holding him prisoner, capturing him inside, hoping his hot need would build anew.

"It's late," he said.

"It's early."

"I don't want to miss the comet."

"Won't there be other comets, Gabriel?"

"Not for seventy years." He disentangled her legs. "Let's get ready, Knickers. I must shave and that takes a while."

"Yes, I know," she said, caressing his jagged scar with her fingertips. "But I always forget."

Since the cabin had only one room, she didn't dare dawdle.

She donned her new gown, marveling at the perfect fit.

Twisting her hair into a braided topknot, she cast fond glances toward the spool bed, the leather-thonged chest, and the dragon-decorated screen, all retrieved from Mama Scarlet's bedroom. Gabriel had paid Madam a small fortune for the items, eager to please the young girl he'd won in a poker game.

"Are you ready?" Gabriel asked, hot to trot.

Men! Always so impatient! Knickers joined him at the door.

Good-bye, chest and screen, she said, silently. *Good-bye, dressing table with your bottles of Creme de Marshmallows and Milk of Cucumber. Good-bye, spool bed. Good-bye, paintings of Mama Scarlet and Beatrice, my pretty baby sister. Good-bye, paintings of me. Good-bye, mirror. Good-bye, reflection. Good-bye, me.*

Chapter Twenty-Eight

While Gabriel saddled Bucket and Dottie, Knickers visited the outhouse.

Then she gazed fearfully at the sky.

Thunder still sounded, but it was a distant echo. Gabriel said that thunder was God's cough.

Knickers loved horses more than anything, except Gabriel, and yet she fervently prayed that Dottie would catch a stone in her hoof. Maybe then Gabriel would turn back. But the dappled gray mare pranced along the trail as if she were trotting on air. So did Bucket, son of Gabriel's mare, Nantucket. When Knickers, curious, had asked about the name, Gabriel had laughed.

"There once was a man from Nantucket," he'd chanted, "who kept all his coins in a bucket. But his daughter, named Nan, ran off with a man, and as for the bucket, Nantucket."

Knickers gave Dottie's neck a few pats, then looked up again. The thunder had hushed, but a herd of clouds grazed, chomping at the sky.

Dottie chomped at the bit.

Knickers felt her eyes almost pop out of her head. Folks might be burrowing in caves elsewhere, but here in Cripple Creek they lined the streets. Two, maybe 300 people. Venders hawked comet pills and weenies on a stick and candy apples. Some even sold bottles of liquor.

"Shame, shame!" she shouted. Prodding Dottie closer to

Bucket, she said, "Those men shouldn't sell demon rum on the street, Gabriel. It's indecent."

"We don't have to buy it, honey."

She held her tongue, even though she had a feeling that the men who bought the whiskey and applejack would soon be drunk and rowdy, if they weren't already. And, oh, how she wanted to go home.

Gabriel stabled the horses at the livery, not far from Johnson's Department Store. "I wish I could stay with Dottie and Bucket," she said.

"Don't be silly, Knickers. The horses will munch stale oats while we dine on thick steaks, fresh snap beans, and snails."

"I'd rather eat oats than snails, Gabriel."

Arm in arm, they joined the crowd around a preacher whose skin had the dark shine of coal. Suddenly, the crowd burst into song, a hymn, "There Is Sunshine in Your Soul." Knickers sang, too, her voice unspoiled by whiskey or tobacco, scrubbed clean by the mountain air.

Gabriel's prideful grin outshone the sun that hovered just above the horizon.

Soon it'll be twilight, Knickers thought, as the hymn ended. *Soon darkness will descend and the dangfool comet will streak across the dangfool sky.*

Wending his way through the crowd, a small black boy waved a sign above his head. Printed letters spelled out: GREAT SHOW AT THE TROPIC. LADIES AND GENTLEMEN INVITED.

"Might we catch the show at the Tropic, Gabriel?"

"Maybe."

After the comet, she thought, echoing his thoughts.

Vivid colors tinted the grazing clouds. Then the sun disappeared below the horizon and Knickers felt her heart resume its normal rhythm.

The sun didn't explode, did it? she chided, silently. *You've got to disremember your fear of sunsets.*

Glancing around, she saw that Myers Avenue was now brightly lit. Mr. Edison's lightbulbs illuminated parlor house windows. Handheld torches flared and streetlamps cast an eerie glow. Overhead, the clouds had drifted away, leaving stars in their wake. If it weren't for the dangfool comet, she could enjoy this wondrous sight, this wondrous night.

She pictured her painting, the one she'd start tomorrow morning, after her bath. She'd use umber, sienna, sepia, add some gray shadows and—

What did a comet look like? Gabriel said it was a moving celestial body with a luminous tail. Celestial, he said, meant heavenly or divine. Divine meant sacred. Sacred meant holy.

Were comets holy?

Folks gave way to Gabriel's crutch, and they soon stood in front of the Old Homestead. Inside, the girls were throwing a party. Knickers heard a piano and the sound of laughter. She sniffed and smelled an all-day roast. She hadn't eaten lunch and beneath her chemise and petticoats, her tummy growled.

A yellow-haired, pasty-faced woman thrust her head through the open, second-story window. "Mary Knickers!" she shouted. "It's been a long time!"

"Hello, Miss Mollie."

"Aw, don't call me miss. You're all grown up. What a pretty gown. I fail to catch your knickers, though. Lord, how that used to rile Scarlet."

"Mama Scarlet always said a girl shouldn't show her undergarments for all the world to see."

"Hullo, Gabriel. You look fit."

"So do you, Miss Mollie."

Knickers watched Mollie preen and pat her wispy yellow braid. Apparently, she'd never discovered the whereabouts of her Princess Hair Restorer. Or, more likely, the dang stuff didn't work.

"Do you still live here," Knickers asked, "at the Homestead?"

"Naw. I'm too old. Got myself a room above the Bucket of Blood Saloon, where the miners don't give a hoot how old you are. Some of them young pups don't want no spring chickens. They'd rather have a whore who's well-seasoned, someone who's on the ball, if ya get my drift." She heehawed. "I'm here for the comet wingding. It's an open invitation, Mary Knickers. Why don't you join us?"

"Gabriel?"

"Sure, honey. Folks'll yell when the comet appears."

Maybe we won't hear them, she thought prayerfully. She entered, then walked toward the second parlor. Immediately, she was surrounded by girls from her past.

"Mary Knickers," one plump girl said, "why ain't you paid us a visit? We were the same age when you left the profession and—"

"I never joined the profession."

"That don't explain why you ain't come callin'."

"I've been occupied."

"Havin' babies?"

"No. Posing for Gabriel's paintings. The Homestead looks the same," she said, wanting to change the subject.

"The piana's new."

Knickers sneaked a peek at the grand piano, where a man dark as chocolate played a ragtime piece. Then her gaze swept the room. The wallpaper had been ordered from Europe. There was an Edison phonograph with its large morning glory speaker. Teakwood tables and banquet lamps shone, the former from polishing, the latter from electricity. She had once thought the Old Homestead handsomely decorated, but tonight its opulence seemed cloying, especially when she compared it to her snug but airy cabin.

"Let's you and me visit the other parlor, Mary Knickers," said the plump girl. "There's food. Puddings, hams, roasts and such. And a cake that looks like a comet." She licked her lips. "Madam plans to serve the cake after the comet."

"Comet, comet, comet! I'm sick and tired of the dangfool comet. If someone says that word one more time, I'll scream. Where's Gabriel?"

"He's probably standing by the door with the other gents. They don't want to miss the com . . . uh, commotion."

Knickers stomped down the hallway. Sure enough, Gabriel stood just inside the entranceway. He leaned on his crutch and smoked his pipe and laughed at something Mollie said. He didn't care that his Knickers was scared out of her wits.

Shoving the other men aside, she brushed past him.

"I'm going home," she called over her shoulder. "If you want to stay, stay. If not, I'll be at the livery, saddling up Dottie." She fisted her hands until her knuckles whitened. "If someone tries to stop me, he'll be puking up teeth."

"Wait! Knickers, wait!" Gabriel yelled.

"I'm tired of waiting," she said.

Outside, the street was a mass of bodies and there were so many lit torches, the sky looked like a sunset.

Two drunken men, one fat, one skinny, reeled toward Knickers. The fat man slanted a glance at the Old Homestead. "Let's you and me get a room, little lady," he said, making an obscene gesture.

The skinny man laughed and said, "You're too drunk, bub. Couldn't get it up if you tried."

"Who ya callin' drunk?"

"You, you bastard."

"Who ya callin' bastard?"

The skinny man jabbed at the fat man's face.

Knickers sensed the fat man's punch before she actually felt it. Holding her chin, she staggered forward, into the street.

After that, everything seemed to happen all at once.

"Knickers, are you all right?" Gabriel yelled.

"I'm fine!" she shouted at the top of her lungs. "Stay where you are!"

"Look at the sky!" a gent hollered.

"The comet!" screamed a lady. "It's falling!"

"I don't want to die," another lady wailed.

"You won't die, you fool," Gabriel said. "The comet isn't falling."

Nobody paid him any heed. As one, the crowd surged down the street, arms flailing, boots stomping everything in their path—including quite a few women who had fainted. Knickers heard the yowl of a dog. Or was it a cat?

Desperate, she lowered her head and butted her way toward Gabriel.

They pressed their bodies against the Old Homestead's wall. Knickers squeezed her eyes shut, but she could still hear the sound of thundering feet. In her mind's eye she could see the crushed form of a dog or cat. Tears brimmed, overflowed. At the same time, she felt happy. Happy that her fears had been without substance. Happy that she was alive. Bruised, but alive.

"And yet, I'd rather have one week, one month, one year with you, Gabriel," she whispered, "than a lifetime without you."

"What did you say, little love? I couldn't hear—"

"Nothing, Gabriel. Just hold me."

"It's over, Knickers. The comet's gone. Open your eyes and dry your tears. Animals got stepped on, but none were killed. Some men are helping the injured. I wouldn't be of any use. The street has more ruts than I care to count."

"Why did they act that way, Gabriel? Why?"

"I don't think folks expected the comet to appear so close to the earth. They failed to remember that Colorado has a very high altitude. Lord almighty, that comet's tail streaked across the night sky. What a sight!"

"What a catastrophe!"

He caressed her chin. "Poor baby. How do you feel?"

"Fine, Gabriel. I'm just glad it's over. I hope the drunk man who hit me got stepped on real hard. I hope he puked his demon rum."

"Knickers!"

"I know. Mama Scarlet wouldn't approve. She always said a true lady should go quietly about her business when on the street. 'Swinging the arms, sucking parasol handles, and talking very loud are all evidence of ill-breeding.' I'm just glad Mama Scarlet didn't witness what happened here tonight."

"I'm sorry *you* did. I should have listened to you."

"No, Gabriel. You saw your dangfool comet and we didn't get harmed. The crows were wrong."

"The crows were only half-wrong. It could have been much worse. You could have been trampled. You could have left me. Please don't leave me."

"I won't, Gabriel, and that's a promise. Let's go home."

"What about your fancy meal?"

"*Home,* Gabriel!"

"Home," he agreed, limping down the street, trying to avoid the ruts.

She wanted to help him, but knew his pride would never allow it. So she merely hummed "High Society," the ragtime piece she'd heard inside the Old Homestead.

Stars glittered overhead and she felt peaceful. She had meant what she'd whispered, after the stampede. She loved Gabriel with all her heart and soul, and if God took her tomorrow she'd die happy.

They had navigated most of Myers Avenue when Knickers heard a woman shout, "It's back! The comet's back!"

"There's no comet." Knickers glanced up at the sky. "What on earth is that madwoman yelling about?"

Gabriel grinned, then gestured toward the small black boy who had earlier interrupted the preacher's harangue. This time the boy held a different sign aloft. Someone had painted a huge comet. Directly beneath it, letters spelled out: HAVE A HOT TIME IN THE OLD TOWN TONIGHT. JOIN THE PARTY AT THE TROPIC.

The sign was attached to a very long stick and the painted comet, realistically rendered, looked as if it hovered several feet overhead.

"It's going to kill us!" the madwoman yelled.

"They should lock her up," Knickers murmured. Amazingly, she heard the sound of thundering feet again. "Gabriel, there's going to be another stampede. Please let me help you. We've got to get out of the way."

Before she could move, a small crowd rounded the corner and raced down the street. "It's going to kill us!" the madwoman repeated, her shoe kicking Gabriel's crutch out from under him.

"Run, Knickers!" he shouted, falling on his back.

For one incredulous moment, she thought he meant the comet, that he was telling her to run from the comet. Then she saw a horse-drawn buckboard. It careened down the street. There was no driver, the wagon was filled with bricks and lumber, and Gabriel lay directly in its path.

"Somebody help us!" she cried, sinking to her knees, tugging at Gabriel's shirt. But the crowd had surged past and the only person left standing was the little boy with the sign for the Tropic. Knickers felt Gabriel's shirt rip beneath her fingers.

"Crawl away," he urged. "Hurry."

"I'll never leave you, never!"

"Knickers, *please!*"

"No."

"Dear God, how can I make you leave?"

"You can't. God can't, either."

"I love you, Knickers, always."

"I love you, Gabriel," she said, covering his body with hers as best she could. But her slight form couldn't protect him from the horse's hooves or the wagon's wheels.

Pressing her cheek against his heart, she heard his heart stop beating. She felt as if stuffed bears crushed her. She knew that at least one hoof had caught her head. She knew that her ribs and legs were broken. But she didn't feel any pain. She knew that she would soon die, but she didn't fear Death. Because she was hugging Gabriel, the only man she had ever wanted, the only man she had ever loved.

A smile creased the corners of her lips and she fisted her small hands. Death wouldn't part her from Gabriel. If Death tried, he'd be puking up teeth.

Chapter Twenty-Nine

"Am I dead?" Hallie asked.

"No."

Gabe loomed above her. He stood, his legs pressed against a bed.

A strange bed. Her bed?

It had to be her bed because she lay on its mattress and her head rested on a pillow. Two pillows. Maybe three.

"You're alive," Gabe said. "And awake. Thank God."

His voice vibrated within the recesses of Hallie's mind, blunting the sharp edge of her terror. And yet, an inexplicable fear clamped her heart, as if her heart had been caught in the jaws of a vise.

She said, "Was I sleeping?"

"I wouldn't exactly call it sleep," Gabe replied. "You passed out. Then you tranced."

"What's the difference?"

"When you trance, your eyes are open."

"I don't remember . . . yes, I do. The wall clunked my head. Where am I?"

"The Imperial Hotel. You've occupied one of their bedrooms for the last forty-five . . ." Gabe looked down at his watch. "Forty-seven minutes. A doctor checked your head, your pulse, even your beautiful ears. You gasped and mumbled something that sounded like 'bread, cheese and wine.' The doctor said aspirin might be more prudent. He pronounced you healthy, wealthy, wise, and stressed."

"I wasn't stressed, Gabe. I was scared. I've never been so scared in my life."

"Me, too. Scared, I mean. After the doctor left, I held your hand and let you trance. I wanted it over, finished, the riddle solved, although I must confess my hand shook. I kept remembering your words when we had our picnic."

"The picnic . . . it rained."

"It didn't rain."

"It didn't?" From her prone position, she gazed up at his face. Then *his* words finally got through to her. "Holy Moses, I've been trancing! Couldn't the doctor see that?"

"Not really. You sounded goofy but normal."

"Define normal."

"You called me Gabriel, which made sense to the doctor. And you kept insisting that you wanted to go home, which made sense to both of us. And you said . . ."

"What? What did I say?"

"You said you hoped the man who hit you would puke his liquor."

"Did he?"

"Yup. I kind of helped him along. After he hit you, I hit him. It was very Charles Bronson, or maybe Clint Eastwood. One punch and he keeled over like a felled tree."

"I feel dizzy, Gabe."

"Of course you do. That drunk bastard's fist caught your stomach. And you sustained a nasty bump on your head."

"Not my stomach. My chin."

"It was your stomach, Hallie."

"Oh, God, I think I'm going to be sick."

Gabe helped her sit up. Then he reached for a flower-decorated bowl. "The doctor warned me," he said, his voice tender, "so I'm all prepared. Unfortunately, the bathroom's down the hall. Everything's the same as it was a hundred years ago, except the mattress. I think the hotel has replaced the mattress. This bowl even has a matching pitcher."

"It's a lovely bowl." She felt her queasy stomach settle, but she couldn't control her tears.

Gabe deposited the bowl on a nearby end table, knelt by the side of the bed, and gathered her into his arms.

"Okay, okay," he crooned. "You're here with me. This isn't a dream." He kneaded the small of her back. "I'm such an idiot, Hallie. You can fly to New York and mull things over. That's reasonable. I have no doubts, none at all, but we've only known each other seven days, even if it feels like a hundred years." He kissed her tousled curls. "You can walk down Myers Avenue till the cows come home."

"We died," she said, her voice catching on a sob. "There was a runaway horse and wagon. And a comet. But the comet was a sign, a stu-stupid sign. Please, Gabe, I want to trance again. Or sleep. Maybe I can change the ending."

"No! The doctor warned me about that, too. He said you might be disoriented for a while, talk gibberish. He said not to let you sleep. He suggested a hospital visit, but your head didn't need any stitches so I said—"

"Please let me sleep."

"Not even close," Gabe teased. "I said I'd watch over you very carefully. Now, dry your tears and stand up. We're going to walk around the room until your head clears completely. You don't like coffee so I ordered some Pepsi from the hotel manager. A six-pack, the kind with caffeine."

"You expect me to drink a six-pack of carbonated caffeine?"

"Yup."

"I'll belch till the cows come home."

"Good. You sound better. Much better."

"If I sound better, why do I have to walk around the room?"

"Stand up, Hallie. I'm not kidding."

Tentatively, she toed the carpet, then stood. Almost immediately, her rebellious body sagged against Gabe.

He circled her waist. "Take it easy, one step at a time."

"Damn sky legs!"

"You didn't fly," he said.

"Yes, I did. I took a flight through time and space."

While they paced up and down the small bedroom, Hallie related the whole tale. Sometimes despair clawed at her composure and the sounds that wended their way up her throat emerged as whimpers or whispers. When they did, Gabe cradled her head against his shoulder and slowed the pace. She tried not to cry again, but couldn't prevent an occasional sob or shudder.

"Knickers dreamed about crows," she concluded, "and I think I dreamed about them, too. Last night."

"You were attacked by a wall, Hallie, not some panic-stricken mob."

"Knickers escaped the mob. It was the horse and buckboard . . ." She hesitated, then said, "I'm glad."

"You're glad she died? Here, have some more Pepsi. Let's walk faster."

"I'm not talking gibberish. I'm glad she died *happy*. And I think I've discovered the answer to my quest, the lesson I was supposed to learn."

"Which is?"

"Later. I'm beginning to feel claustrophobic. This room is so tiny." Seated on the edge of the bed, she tugged on her boots. "Let's walk outside. Please?"

"Sure. I want to retrieve my Nikon from the car. It's my most prized possession, except for you."

"I'm not a possession."

"That's not what I meant, and you know it."

"Say what you mean, Gabe."

"You're my most prized . . . treasure. I love you, Hallie."

"I love you, too." Her face scrunched. "Why retrieve your camera? Aren't we driving back to Colorado Springs?"

"I've taken this room for the night, if you want to stay. I'm asking, not telling."

"Relax, Gabe. That's a great idea."

After retrieving his camera and two heavy sweatshirts, they strolled down Myers Avenue. The stars shone and the wind hummed a lullaby.

Hallie's gaze lingered on the paved streets. There were a few ruts, but they were caused by tires, not heavy boots or wagon wheels, and the Old Homestead looked much smaller, as if it had shrunk over the years, like an old lady.

"It's hard to believe that this was once the scene of such utter madness," she said. "The sky looked like a sunset, filled with smoky flames from dozens and dozens of torches. People stampeded like cattle. I'm fairly certain I won't ever paint cows again." She shivered.

"What was the answer to your quest, honey?"

She gave him a lopsided grin. "Men! Always so impatient."

"Tell me."

"Okay." She leaned against the Old Homestead's wall. "Love isn't delivered to your door, Gabe. It's not a letter. It's not a neatly wrapped package. Sometimes you have to search a long time . . ." Her dimple flickered. "Sometimes you have to kiss a lot of *basted* frogs before you find your prince." She nibbled at her lower lip. "When you find happiness, you must grab it, relish it, never let it go."

"I couldn't agree more."

"Knickers didn't have a TV or magazine ads or movies,"

Hallie continued, "so she didn't have any preconceived notions about the perfect man. She simply followed her heart. She said . . . before she died, she said, 'I'd rather spend one week, one month, one year with you, Gabriel, than a lifetime without you.' That's one hell of a lesson to learn."

"I've learned it, too, Hallie. For the last week I've followed my heart, but it stopped beating when I lost you."

"You didn't lose me."

"When you said we should wait, I thought I'd lost you. Then, when the wall hit your head, I wanted to go back in time. Not a hundred years. Back to this morning. You were right, Hallie. I should have shared my good news, asked how you felt, discussed your fears rationally. At the very least, I should have asked you to marry me."

She felt a warm glow spread throughout her body. Up until this very moment, she hadn't realized how much she wanted to hear those two words—*marry me.*

"I'll marry you," she said. "I don't care if we live in Washington, D.C. or Transylvania, next door to your fellow vampires. I don't care if you sit in our living room or span the globe. Let's travel together whenever possible, have lots of babies, and live happily ever after. Starring Gabriel Q and Alice W. O'Brien."

"Alice W. O'Brien Quinn."

There was so much joy in his voice, she wanted to capture his words and shove them into her pocket, save them for a rainy day.

But her dress and sweatshirt didn't have pockets, she thought pragmatically.

"Okay, Alice W.," Gabe said, his expression very serious. "The time has come to confess."

"Confess what?"

"Your middle name."

"Look at the stars, Gabe. There must be a million—"

"Your middle name, Hallie."

She heaved a deep sigh. "My mom had this thing for Lewis Carroll, and she loved the name Alice. Since my dad couldn't think of a singer, a woman singer—"

"Wonderland. Your middle name is Wonderland."

"No. White Rabbit."

"Alice White Rabbit O'Brien?"

"When the Jefferson Airplane recorded 'White Rabbit,' parents were naming their kids River and Rainbow and Starshine and—"

"That's great, Hallie. White Rabbit. It's so cute, so cuddly, so you."

"It wasn't me before we met." She auditioned a smile. "I wasn't cuddly."

"My pragmatic bunny," Gabe said, his voice tender.

"There's a six-pack inside our room . . . half a six-pack. Maybe we should return to the hotel and get drunk on Pepsi."

"I don't need carbonated caffeine. *You* intoxicate me, Alice White Rabbit O'Brien Quinn." Squinting through the lens of his camera, he shot a picture.

"Wait," Hallie said. "I didn't have time to pose."

"I didn't have time to focus. But I'm sure the picture will come out fine."

"Just like us."

"The hotel," he urged, grabbing her hand.

Once they were safely inside the tiny room, she could hardly unzip his slacks fast enough. "Now!" she cried, wild to have him.

"Hold your horses, my love. Treasures must be savored."

She saw that his eyes were lazy-lidded with desire. She fell back, onto the mattress. Laughing, he took off his clothes, then her boots, dress, panty hose and undies. Straddling her hips, his hands cupped her breasts, his fingers massaging her nipples through her bra. With a gasp, she reached up and thrust her first finger between his lips. Sucking her finger, he unsnapped her bra. Then he released her finger and slowly drew the bra straps down her arms. It brought to mind their first night of love, only this time she didn't shy away. Instead, she encouraged his entry by digging her heels into the mattress, boosting herself.

"Women," he managed, his voice raspy. "Always so impatient."

"I'm not impatient and I can prove it." Lowering her butt, her hand caressed between his legs.

Gabe caught his breath, but he let her play. His legs trembled and sweat beaded his brow. He heard her say, "If the president sends you someplace I can't go, you'll have to pack some boudoir photos."

"That's easy," he managed to reply. "I have albums galore."

"Boudoir photos of me, you featherbrained mooncalf."

"Deal." He adjusted her position so that she lay on her belly. He let his hands slowly travel down the smooth curve of her back until he molded her buttocks. It was a form of tender revenge for her previous action, massaging his erection, but he soon realized that any retaliation exacted his own pound of flesh. Okay, so it wasn't a pound. But it felt like a pound, powerfully engorged, a salute that rivaled any salute he had ever experienced.

Delighted by her involuntary moan, he heard his own moan. He turned her over and wedged himself between her thighs. Three hard strokes brought him to an intense climax, yet he was blissfully aware that her second climax followed his.

Hallie twined her legs about Gabe's waist, holding him

prisoner, capturing him inside, hoping his hot need would build anew. It did, and she was vainly triumphant when he cried out for the second time.

Her gaze touched upon the window.

“Gabe, it’s raining,” she said. “We’ve lost the stars.”

“No, my love. We’ve found the stars.”

Chapter Thirty

The next morning the rain turned to snow, but only after Gabe had driven back to Colorado Springs.

Barefoot, clothed in her comfy jeans and striped turtleneck, Hallie took a deep breath, clutched the receiver tightly, and placed her long-distance call.

While she waited for her mom or dad to answer, she glanced around the family room. Gabe had enlarged last night's photo and it now occupied the place of honor above the fireplace mantel.

She looked so damn—Knickers would say "dang"—childish, Hallie thought. Gabe's orange and blue Denver Broncos sweatshirt fell below her knees, hiding any assets she might possess. And yet, her face looked happy. No. Ecstatic. Maybe she'd grow her hair long, like Knickers.

"Hi, Mom," Hallie said, upon hearing her mother's cheerful hello.

"Well, it's about time," Josie said. "*Your* daughter finally calls, Shamus, the very same day she's flying home. Your father's standing next to me, Hallie."

"I'm not flying home, Mom. I've canceled my flight."

"Your daughter canceled her flight, Shamus. We figured you might, darling. We've been watching the Weather Channel. All that snow . . . what, Shamus? Your father wants to know if you solved your mystery, Hallie. So do I."

"Yes." She narrated the Knickers-Gabriel story. Gabe placed a mug of herbal tea in her hand so that she could pause, sip, continue. When she finished, there was silence at the other end of the line.

"Mom, are you still there? Gabe, I think I've been disconnected."

"We haven't been disconnected," Josie said. "In fact, *you're* connected."

"What do you mean?"

"Remember Granny Bea?"

"Of course."

"She was Mary's sister."

"*What?*"

"It's true, darling. Her adoptive parents kept it a secret."

Hallie would have dropped her mug, had Gabe not snatched it from her hand. Clutching the receiver tightly with both hands, she said, "Why would they keep it a secret?"

"Remember the times, darling. It was the turn of the century. Today one practically brags about illegitimate offspring, but back then folks tucked it away inside the proverbial closet. It was a family skeleton, a big one. Granny Bea's mother eventually let the cat out of the bag. It was inevitable. Bea had been very naughty and her mother scolded her with something like, 'After all, you're the daughter of a wicked woman.' Or maybe she said woman of ill-repute. Or maybe she called Bea a whore's daughter. In any case, the chastisement backfired. Bea was delighted. Throughout the years, she probed her adoptive mother for more details." Josie sighed. "Bea was always such a free spirit."

"How did *you* find out, Mom?"

"Granny Bea told me. She considered me a free spirit, too, and recognized my love for history. What's that, Shamus? Of course I love you better than history. Sometimes men are so insecure, Hallie, like little boys. Where was I?"

"Granny Bea confessed."

"Right. But she swore me to secrecy. Anyway, I couldn't tell you even if I wanted to. You've always been so straitlaced. No, Shamus, strait*laced,* not straight-*faced.* Apparently, our daughter has developed a sense of humor that won't quit. In fact, she's laughing as we speak."

"Sorry, Mom. Granny Bea was Mary Knickers's baby sister. That's unbelievable. Hey, wait a sec. When I called you from Marianne's, you said you had never heard of the Homestretch. Why did you fib?"

"I didn't fib. Bea's parents knew about Mary Knickers, but they didn't know the name of the parlor house. The adoption was very complicated and very illegal. Knickers handed Bea over to a wealthy miner and his wife. After a few days the miner's wife decided she didn't want a baby, after all. She gave Bea to a lady who was heading east. That greedy lady had once lived next door to Bea's parents. She knew they couldn't have children and desperately wanted them, so she sold Bea—"

"*Sold* Granny Bea?"

"I told you it was illegal. The greedy lady collected five hundred dollars, then took off for parts unknown. By the time Bea learned about her background, Mary Knickers was dead."

"I'm glad I didn't learn about Granny Bea from you, Mom."

"Why, darling?"

"Because my paintings started a quest, which led me to Colorado, which led to my honorable solution."

"Honorable solution?"

"I never considered my paintings honorable, but they are. I paint from the heart, even my dumb cows. I express how I feel, deep down inside." Her gaze touched upon Gabe. "Love is honorable, too, and honest . . . if you love the right person. I think Knickers was reaching out from the past, reaching out across time and space."

"Granted, but I don't understand why she would do that."

"For what it's worth, Mom, here's my theory. Knickers couldn't have babies, and yet she had the perfect love. I think she wanted me to have both—babies *and* love."

"You're in love? Shamus, our daughter's in love. Is that why you canceled your flight?"

"Yes. In fact, my fiancé and I are leaving for Washington tonight, assuming the runways are cleared. Washington, D.C. is where we'll live. My fiancé wants me to find an apartment. Or a rental house. Eventually, we'll build our own house and I'll decorate it. My fiancé says the sky's the limit." She caught Gabe's amused glare. "But I don't need lots of perfect, unique things, Mom, not anymore. I don't care if we eat off chipped plates or sleep inside a bedroll. I'll probably be traveling a lot, visiting different countries. My fiancé," she said for the fourth time, savoring the word, "wants to meet you, attend my gallery opening. Then we'll get married."

"Congratulations, darling."

"You don't sound surprised."

"I'm not. It's Joshua Quinn, isn't it?"

"No, Mom, it's Joshua's brother. Gabe Quinn. Gabriel Q," she added, unable to resist the brag. After all, she was part Irish.

"Gabriel Q? The photojournalist? Shamus, our daughter's about to marry a very famous photographer. Grandchildren! Neil takes a few snapshots when I nag, but you'll send us dozens of pictures, hundreds of pictures. After all, your husband-to-be is a photog—"

"Whoa, Mom. Please don't talk grandkids yet. Give me nine months."

"Nine months," Josie agreed. "Are you sure about your feelings for Gabe, darling?"

"Absolutely positively sure. Holy Moses, Mom. We're running up a phone bill that could pay off the national debt. And I've got to economize, now that Gabe works for the president."

"The president of what?"

"I'll explain during our next phone call, or save it for Marianne. Give Daddy a kiss for me."

"Shamus, our daughter wants me to kiss you. No, silly, after I hang up. Men! Always so impatient. Talk at you soon, Hallie."

"Very soon. Bye, Mom."

"Bye Mom," Gabe said into the receiver, just before he hung it up.

"That was mean. My mother will want to 'talk at you.' So will my dad. He'll probably give you the third degree. But all you really have to do is tell him about Napkin and Eartha Kitt and he'll forget the rest of his questions."

Gabe held her at arm's length. "You're absolutely positively sure about what?"

"Love and laughter and happily ever after." Walking over to the fireplace, she saluted the happy portrait above its mantel. A hand salute, of course, not a special Gabe salute.

Speaking of salutes . . .

Making an about-face, she said, "Come here, Drac. I vant to kiss you till the cows come home."

"I don't have any cows, little love. I live in an area with covenants."

"Bullragged jellyfish! Don't be so pragmatic. Maybe they'll change the covenents. Maybe they'll even change them before we finish kissing."

"Hallie, you're adorable."

"Am I really?"

"Yup."

"Cross my heart," they both said together.

Then, together, they reached for each other's hearts.

About the Author

Denise Dietz is the best-selling author of several novels, including *Footprints in the Butter, An Ingrid Beaumont Mystery Costarring Hitchcock the Dog*—and the highly acclaimed historical romance, *Dream Dancer.* She has been a journalist, worked for Paramount as an extra, and is an avid Denver Broncos fan. Denise lives on Vancouver Island with her husband, novelist Gordon Aalborg, and her mostly Norwegian elkhound, Pandora. She likes to hear from readers. You can email her from her Web site: www.denisedietz.com.